SERPENT IN PARADISE

Shafinur Ali

Katal Khair

Dirt Sylhet

Bengladesh

It was the answer to Teri's prayers when elderly Mrs Emma Roland offered her a job and a home near Cape Town. But what business was it of Sloan Garfield's? Why did he have to be so hostile and suspicious? And why couldn't Teri get him out of her mind?

SERPENT IN PARADISE

BY

ROSEMARY CARTER

MILLS AND BOON LIMITED
15–16 BROOK'S MEWS
LONDON W1A 1DR

First published 1983
Australian copyright 1983
Philippine copyright 1983
This edition 1983

© Rosemary Carter 1983

ISBN 0 263 74446 9

Set in Monophoto Plantin 10 on 11 pt.
01—1283 — 53989

Made and printed in Great Britain by
Richard Clay (The Chaucer Press) Ltd,
Bungay, Suffolk

CHAPTER ONE

TERI glanced at her watch and saw that it was even later than she had realised. Her lunch-hour was half over and she still had to get to the supermarket before popping in to Mrs Roland.

It was the storm that had delayed her. Tropical thunderstorms were always to be reckoned with in Johannesburg in the summer. There had been one each day for the last week, always in the late afternoon, when the traffic out of the city was at its busiest. This storm had erupted unexpectedly, and Teri, caught in open-toed sandals and without an umbrella, had had to shelter beneath the wide awning of a shop-front until the worst of the downpour had abated.

She grimaced as water squelched in her shoes, and just for a moment she wondered if she had been foolish not to go back to the library without visiting Mrs Roland. Emma Roland would have understood. But she would have been disappointed. With her twisted ankle keeping her temporarily immobile, she was depending on the groceries that Teri had promised to bring her.

She was not far from Mrs Roland's flat now, and across the road was the supermarket. Teri usually crossed the road at the traffic lights, but they were some distance away; with her sandals waterlogged and uncomfortable she decided to jaywalk.

She had just stepped off the kerb when she saw the car turning in to angle-park. She took a hasty step backwards, but she was not quick enough to escape the rush of muddy water stirred up by the tyres, and a swirl of it hit her dress.

It *would* be the one good dress she possessed! she
thought, throwing a furious look at the car. It was
silver-grey, long and sleek and expensive-looking. For
some reason its elegance served only to enrage her
further. Without thinking she bent, picked up a ball of
mud and hurled it at the car. The sight of the mud
spattered on the shining chrome gave her a moment of
intense and gleeful satisfaction.

She had reached the opposite kerb when she felt a
hand close on her arm, and spinning round, she found
herself looking up, quite a long way up, into a pair of
intensely blue eyes, and she felt the oddest quiver. She
had never seen a face that was so handsome, nor quite
so self-assured. Thick fair hair was vivid against a deep
tan, and the lines of a hard mouth and chin combined
in an unusual mixture of power and sensuousness.

Fear was delayed, coming seconds later than it
normally would have done. This was not one of the
more desirable parts of the city, strangers were not to
be taken lightly. What did he want of her? In sudden
panic Teri glanced sideways, wondering if anyone
would come to her aid if she screamed.

'I won't harm you.' The blue eyes were mocking, as
if he understood the gist of her thoughts. 'I'm the
owner of that car.' He made a small gesture. 'Why did
you chuck mud at me?'

'You dirtied my dress,' she said, thinking that his
dark suit and silk shirt went well with the car. Both
had the same look of money and elegance.

His eyes left her face and descended to the dress.
There was something blatant in the way that he
studied it, as if he was seeing through the garment to
the shapely figure it clothed. Teri's earlier outrage
returned.

'A pretty dress,' was all he said.

'It happens to be the only one I possess.' Not true,

but not wildly over-exaggerated either.

'You were jaywalking,' he pointed out mildly.

'My sandals were wet through and the traffic-lights are a million miles away. You must have seen me.'

'Actually I didn't.'

'You could have let me pass anyway. Did nobody ever teach you to be considerate?'

'Illogical and a virago.' The corners of his lips lifted. 'At worst I was looking for an apology. At best I thought you might offer to clean off the mess you made. I certainly didn't expect an attack.'

Teri drew herself up to her full height—five feet and six inches seemed oddly small beside what was surely six feet two of leanly muscled manhood. 'You must be crazy if you thought I'd do either! May I have my arm back—I'm in a hurry.'

She was walking away when she heard him chuckle. For a moment she was tempted to turn so that she could see how the autocratic face looked when it was amused, but pride stopped her just in time. Stiffening her shoulders, she squelched her way with as much dignity as she could into the supermarket.

'You look as if the weight of the world rests on those slender shoulders,' a smiling voice remarked.

'That bad, Andy?' Teri was rueful. 'I was caught in the storm, and then I was splashed by a car—the most arrogant man you ever met!' The last words were said on a burst of passion.

'You know him?' The young man regarded her quizzically.

'We exchanged words,' Teri said carefully. 'You see, I'd revenged myself by throwing mud at his car.'

Andy laughed affectionately. 'Little mischief!'

'He called me a virago. You should have seen him—tall, well-dressed, the kind who's convinced he's

God's gift to women. He had the gall to think I owed
him an apology.'

'He seems to have made quite an impression on you.'

'A bad one,' Teri said firmly. 'Just look at this dress!'

'It will wash out, won't it? What's bothering you,
love? It's not like you to get so upset over a bit of
mud.'

'I *am* over reacting.' She took a breath. 'I heard this
morning that the rent of the flat has gone up.'

'You were going to ask for a raise.'

'I did—and didn't get one.' She frowned. 'And I'm
worried about Jill. She's not looking well.'

'There is an answer for you and your young sister.'
Teri looked up quickly. 'Andy . . .'

'You know I want to marry you. I earn a decent
wage here at the supermarket.'

'Don't go on,' she said gently.

'I could take care of you both.'

'I know you could, and you're a darling to suggest
it. I'm so fond of you, Andy, you know that, but don't
tempt me—I don't want to marry you for the wrong
reasons.'

'The right ones—if you'd let them be.' For once
Andy looked serious. 'I won't pester you, love, not
between the sugar and the oranges. Let's go out for
dinner tonight.'

'Oh, Andy, thank you, but I don't think so. I
should be with Jill.' Teri glanced at her watch. 'Just
look at the time! Mrs Roland must be wondering if I
got lost. I just popped in here to get her some
groceries.'

'You've been really good to her,' Andy remarked.

'She has no one else.'

'Lucky for her that you happened to be around
when she fell. You've been pretty marvellous to her
ever since.'

'I like her,' Teri said simply. 'She's sweet, and so very lonely. I must run, Andy, I know Mrs Roland is waiting for me, and I don't want to be late getting back to work.'

Andy's offer of marriage was more tempting than he realised, Teri reflected, as she walked in the direction of Emma Roland's flat. The young assistant manager of the supermarket had all the qualities a husband should have. He was a fine person, kind and considerate. Dependable. A man to rely on in a crisis. And his affection for her was genuine.

Marriage to Andy would bring solutions. No more worries about rent and food. More time with Jill, time that could be spent out of doors. Sunshine and fresh air were what Jill needed.

There were so many reasons why marriage to Andy made good sense. And one reason why it made no sense at all. She did not love him. He was nice, he was also just a little boring.

Unbidden an image came into her mind—a tall lean man with a gauntly handsome face and mocking eyes. Arrogant and doubtless very opinionated. But exciting with it.

Thrusting him from her mind, Teri wondered why she had given a moment's thought to the nameless stranger who had made her so angry. That kind of man was not for her. He would move in an opulent world very different from hers. She could see him surrounded by hordes of sophisticated women, all eager for his attention.

The very worst sort of man, and quite definitely not for her. When she did get married it probably would be to Andy or to someone very like him. And that would be the end of a passion she dimly perceived in herself but had never experienced. Cursing herself for

the rebellious streak that said there must be more to
life than security and dependability, she kicked her
foot at a puddle of rainwater and turned into the
building where Emma Roland lived.

After ringing the bell twice with no response, she
tried the door and found it open. 'Mrs Roland, it's me,
Teri,' she called with a cheerfulness that belied a tinge
of apprehension. It was unlike the elderly woman not
to be at the door to welcome her. Perhaps her ankle
was giving her trouble today?

'In here, dear,' came an answering voice.

Teri paused in the kitchen to put down the
groceries, then went into the living-room. 'Sorry I'm
so late, but . . .' She stopped in shock. Standing by the
window, one long leg extended carelessly across the
other, was her stranger.

'Hello, dear, I want you to meet Mr Garfied. Sloan,
this is Miss Malloy.'

'How do you do, Miss Malloy.' The low voice was
bland, with no sign of recognition.

So that was the way he wanted to play it. Crossing
the room, Teri held out her hand. His eyes flickered—
she had taken him by surprise, she thought, and was
satisfied for the second time that day—but the hand
that took hers in return was calm and unhurried. His
fingers were cool, the handshake firm.

'How do you do, Mr Garfield,' Teri said pertly, and
wondered why she could not control the sudden racing
of her pulses.

Withdrawing a hand that felt as if it was burning,
she turned to Mrs Roland with what she hoped was an
air of indifference. 'I've left the groceries in the
kitchen.'

'That's kind of you.'

Caught by a note of strain, Teri looked at Emma
Roland, really looked at her for the first time since she

had entered the room. It must have been her shock on
seeing Sloan Garfield that had prevented her from
noticing her friend's strain, she realised now. Mrs
Roland's face was a little pale, and her eyes lacked
their usual sparkle. Come to think of it, there was a
sense of strain in the room itself, in the atmosphere.

'Mrs Roland, are you all right?' she asked anxiously.

'Quite all right.'

She was *not* all right. Teri knew that quite certainly.
Casting a glance at the hard taut figure by the window,
she put an impulsive hand on the elderly woman's
arm. 'Something's wrong, isn't it?'

'No, Teri, you're imagining things.' Mrs Roland
allowed herself a brief smile. 'But why don't you drop
by a little later?'

A dismissal, though gently put. Sloan Garfield
remained silent, but on his face was an expression
which seemed to warn that angels would not tread the
ground on to which Teri was now trespassing.

Cheeks warm, she hesitated a moment longer. It was
not her imagination that Emma Roland was upset, and
that Mr Garfield had something to do with it. But Mrs
Roland was not about to confide the cause of her
distress, that was clear enough, and Teri did not have
the right to insist that she did.

'Thank you.' She gave a bright smile. 'I'll come if I
can.'

She looked at the arrogant stranger again. This time
it was her turn to let an expression take the place of
words. The tilt of her chin proclaimed a warning of
her own. 'Don't try any trouble or you'll have me to
reckon with.' Aloud she said politely, 'So nice to have
met you, Mr Garfield.'

Teri did not visit Emma Roland that evening.
Arriving home from work in the late afternoon she

found that Jill was not well. Her two-year-old sister
was asleep in the big rattan armchair belonging to her
baby-sitter, Louise Miles. The small face was flushed,
the cheeks hot to Teri's touch, and she stirred
restlessly, giving a cough that shook the small body.

'She's been like this all day,' Louise said.

'Poor little mite! No sooner does she get over one
infection than she starts another. I wish I knew what
to do, Louise.'

'I'd take her to the park more often, fresh air is what
she needs, but I don't have the time.' Apart from
looking after Jill while Teri worked, Louise was the
caretaker of the building, and her duties kept her busy.

'I know, and you're a darling to look after her for
me at all. I wish I had more time for Jill. As it is'—a
worried frown creased Teri's forehead—'I may have
to start moonlighting.'

'The rent?'

'Right. It really is going up, then?'

'Afraid so.' Louise grimaced. 'What will you do?'

'I can probably get an evening job cataloguing
books.' Teri gave a little laugh. 'Andy asked me again
to marry him.'

'Perhaps you should consider it.'

As he had done once before, Sloan Garfield invaded
Teri's mind. Wretched man! They had barely
exchanged three sentences, why did she keep thinking
of him! She gave her head a violent shake.

Louise was amused. 'I like Andy.'

'I like him too,' Teri said, without explaining. 'But
it wouldn't be fair to marry him.'

'How will you manage?'

Teri looked across at Jill. Poor baby! Had their
beloved parents not perished in a boating accident,
Jill's life would be so different. The lovely fun-loving
mother, who at forty had been young enough to have a

baby twenty years after the birth of her first daughter, would have devoted her days to her. Perhaps the rambling old house with its wooded garden would not have been sold after all. Teri remembered the happiness of her own childhood in that garden.

'I'll have to manage,' she said slowly.

'Don't be too hard on yourself.' Louise's words were unexpected. As Teri jerked up to look at her, she went on, 'It's not the first time I've seen that pensive mood in your face, and I know what it means. You've done your best for Jill.'

'I want to see her well. I want to see some colour in her cheeks, and I don't mean a flush brought on by fever. I want her to build up some resistance against these endless infections. I want to give her a secure home.'

'It will all happen,' Louise soothed.

Words. Words came cheaply. But Teri knew them to be well-meant, and she drew comfort from them.

'It *will* happen,' she agreed with sudden fierceness. 'Don't ask me how, Louise, but it will. Thanks for looking after Jill.'

Gently, so as not to waken her, she lifted the little girl into her arms and carried her up two flights of stairs to her own flat.

It was almost a week before Teri had a chance to visit Emma Roland again. The days had been busy. In addition to her normal library hours, she was now working an evening shift. It was work she enjoyed, and she was thankful of the chance to earn money to pay the increased rent, but her time with Jill was even more limited than before.

The little girl was still coughing, and her face was tired and wan. Louise, a gem of a friend, took her for the odd walk, but what Jill needed was several hours at

a time out of doors. They would go picnicking over
the weekend, Teri decided. Perhaps Mrs Roland
would join them. She had a feeling the elderly woman
would enjoy the outing.

'What a lovely idea,' was Emma Roland's response
to the invitation. 'You're a kind girl, Teri—helping a
stranger in a supermarket, continuing to befriend her.'

'Anyone else would have done the same,' Teri
protested, a little embarrassed, though warmed by the
compliment.

'I'm not so sure.'

'You'll join us?' Teri changed the subject.

'I'd love to.' Emma put down her tea-cup. 'And I
have a question for you too, my dear, one I want you
to consider very carefully before giving me an answer.'

Caught by the seriousness in her tone, Teri looked
up curiously. There was something different about her
friend today. She had noticed it from the moment
she'd entered the flat. Now she wondered what was
coming.

'I've decided to leave here.'

'Oh no!' In the moment of disappointment Teri
realised how fond she had become of Emma Roland.

'I'm going to the Cape. I want you to come too,
Teri. You and Jill.'

Green eyes were troubled. 'I don't think I can do
that.'

'I don't expect you just to pack up and leave here on
the strength of a simple request. Let me fill you in,
Teri.'

Emma Roland picked up a photo album which had
been lying on the table, in readiness for this moment,
Teri realised. She turned a few pages, then handed the
open album across to the girl with the words, 'Vins
Doux.'

'Vins Doux,' Teri repeated wonderingly, as she

looked down at two photographs of a great white house set against a lushly green setting.

'French for sweet wines,' she heard Emma say. 'A wine estate, Teri.'

'That's where you're going?'

'Yes.'

'It's beautiful.'

'The photos don't do it justice. The reality is even lovelier. Well, Teri, what do you think?'

'You're going there on a holiday?'

'To live. Vins Doux is my home.'

Teri looked again at the house with its gracious Cape Dutch architecture and its spectacular setting, and wondered why anyone with such a home would willingly have chosen to live in one of Johannesburg's drearier suburbs. Willingly? Perhaps Mrs Roland had been forced to leave Vins Doux. Perhaps it was many years since she had lived there at all. For the first time it occurred to Teri that she knew very little about the woman who had become her friend.

'I think you'd be happy at Vins Doux.'

'It's not that simple. This is my home. I can't just leave it.'

'It hasn't been much of a home since your parents died,' Emma said gently.

Teri met her gaze steadily. 'I'm trying to make it one.'

'You have great courage, I know. You'd love the Cape, Teri.'

'I'm sure I would. But you haven't told me why you want me to come with you.'

'I want a companion.'

A quick glance at the foot that had twisted on a slick of oil in the supermarket. Was it giving its owner even more trouble than Teri had realised?

'I don't have any nursing experience,' she said tentatively.

'You don't need any. I've been very lonely since my husband died. There are times when I feel low, when I really need a friend. I've grown very fond of you both, you and Jill. Come to Vins Doux with me; you'll have a home and I'll have company.'

'I don't know. . . .'

'Jill would love it. We're close to the sea, she'd have a marvellous time.'

Green eyes sparkled. 'You're twisting my arm!'

'Ah, that's good. You haven't breathed till you've breathed the Cape air, Teri. Jill would thrive on it.'

'Wretched woman!' Teri gave a little laugh. 'I didn't know you could be so beguiling.'

She got to her feet and went to the window. Below her the view was one of concrete buildings and busy traffic. A Highveld wind whipped around a corner, stirring up dust and old newspapers. Some of South Africa's loveliest suburbs were in this city, gardens where flowers and shrubs grew in colourful profusion, but this was not one of them. The view from her own flat was no different.

In the year that had passed since the death of their parents she had tried very hard to create a new life for Jill and herself. Their father's once-thriving business had fallen on hard times, and when all the creditors had been appeased there had been little money left. Teri had tried to make a new home, yet in a sense Emma Roland was right. It was nothing like the home they had once had. What the flat lacked most of all perhaps was a sense of belonging, of roots.

'Do you feel you would be giving up too much?' she heard Mrs Roland ask.

'My friends. My job.'

Louise was a dear friend. Andy too, despite the fact that she did not reciprocate the feelings he felt for her. Her job was one she enjoyed. She had worked hard to become a librarian, working with books meant very much to her.

'Give yourself time to think,' Emma said. 'I don't need an answer today.'

Wise lady. Shrewd too. She must know that her offer was tempting. A breathing-space in which she need not worry about rent and food, a chance to let Jill enjoy sea-air and a garden. A wonderful chance—the kind of chance that comes along only once.

She turned from the window. 'I'll come with you.'

'Oh, Teri, I'm so glad!' Emma beamed.

'I'll need some time, though. For one thing, I can't just walk out of my job.'

'I have things to settle here too. A month, Teri?'

'Perfect.' Leaving the window, she came over to Emma and gave her a hug. 'You're a darling for asking me.'

She picked up the open album, and looked again at the photos. Incredible to think that this beautiful house would soon be her home. Suddenly she was very excited.

It was only when she stood up to go that a thought came to her and she turned to her friend. 'Last time I was here I met a man, a Mr Garfield. Forgive me, Mrs Roland, but does he have something to do with your decision?'

Emma smiled. 'It was my decision to go to Vins Doux. It's time to go back.'

'Buy yourself some nice clothes.'

Disbelievingly Teri took in the amount on the cheque Emma had just handed her. Eyes wide, she looked up. 'I can't take this!'

'And some clothes for Jill.'

'I can't do this. . . .'

Emma was smiling. 'And if that's not enough, tell me, and I'll write out another cheque.'

Teri shook her head. 'I have clothes.'

'You take very good care of the things you have, but I think it's been a long while since you had anything new.'

'You're ashamed of me,' Teri said in a low voice.

'No, my dear, I could never be that. But you deserve a new wardrobe, and you'll feel much happier at Vins Doux if you have one.'

Not for the first time in the three days since Teri had agreed to be Mrs Roland's companion did she wonder what she was going to.

'It's a lot of money,' she said now.

'No more than I can afford. Go on a shopping spree, Teri, and enjoy it.'

It seemed there was no end to the surprises her friend was beginning to spring on her. Judging by the way she lived and dressed, Teri had taken Emma Roland to be a woman of modest means. That a wine estate in the Cape was her home had been astonishing news. The cheque was generosity she had never expected.

Enjoy a shopping spree, Emma had commanded, and once Teri had become used to the idea that the money was hers to spend, she did just that. She possessed an eye for fashion and colour which she had never been able to indulge in before now. It was bliss to walk into shops whose windows she had previously only gazed at. Fun to try on garments, to plan and co-ordinate. Fun to buy. It was a joy to fit Jill out with new clothes.

'I feel like Cinderella,' she laughed, when she showed her purchases to Mrs Roland.

'With a difference,' said that woman. 'When the clock strikes midnight your clothes won't turn to rags.'

It was all like a dream. 'I keep wondering when I will wake out of it,' Teri said to Louise and Andy.

'It's a dream I could bear to live with,' Louise laughed, but Andy put in sadly, 'I have a feeling we'll never see you again.'

'Nonsense,' Teri protested fiercely. 'Mrs Roland needs a companion for a while. It isn't a permanent arrangement. She won't want me for ever.'

She had not known that time could pass so quickly. As the Boeing left the ground on its way to the Cape it was hard to believe that a month had actually passed since the day when she had first seen the photos of Vins Doux. Teri tried to answer Jill's questions—the little girl was enraptured by the plane—and she knew that her own excitement matched her sister's.

They landed in Cape Town to yet another surprise. Waiting to meet them was a man in immaculate uniform who spoke deferentially to Mrs Roland, calling her 'madam', and who led them to a sparkling Rolls-Royce in the parking-ground. The man's name was Johan, and it seemed he was employed as a chauffeur at Vins Doux. Teri was awed by his haughty demeanour, but Emma was her usual self, friendly and unaffected. Yet as if she had been speaking to chauffeurs and riding in Rolls-Royces all her life, Teri realised. That, perhaps, was the biggest surprise of all.

She was all at once very glad of the clothes she had bought. She knew now that she would need them.

A slight nervousness at the thought of the place she was coming to faded as the car left the airport. She had known that the Cape Peninsula would be beautiful, but the loveliness that she saw on all sides was more breathtaking than anything she had expected.

There was the grandeur of Table Mountain, its flat top suitably bedecked in its tablecloth of white cloud, and the summits called Lion's Head and Devil's Peak flanking it on either side.

'It's every postcard I've ever seen,' Teri said, awed, and Emma laughed.

And then they had left Table Mountain behind them and there were other mountains. They rose on one side of the road, their slopes wooded and sweet-smelling. On the other side the land fell away steeply to an ocean that was a deep prussian blue with a white line of foam where the waves hurled themselves with wild abandon on to the rocks.

Mrs Roland sat in front with Johan. They were talking, but Teri did not take in a word that was said. She wound down the window, and then she put Jill on her lap and showed her the ocean and the waves, and, most exciting of all, a fishing trawler making its way back to port. The air that wafted in through the window was a potent composite of mountain shrubs and ocean saltiness. Teri drew in long breaths of it, and as she looked at the pale cheeks of her small sister she thought that Jill could not fail to get strong here.

The car took the road with purring smoothness, but Teri registered its luxuriousness only abstractedly. She was far too busy pointing things out to Jill—the wild flowers that dotted the scrub, a lagoon, a deserted stretch of beach, another boat, a very big one this time, on its way to distant shores.

And then they were turning inland, and the scenery changed. 'Wine country,' said Emma, turning in her seat with a smile.

'Is it far to Vins Doux?'

'We're nearly there.'

Wine country indeed. They drove through lush green valleys, and wherever the eye could see there were vineyards. Teri gazed out of the window entranced.

'Stop the car, please, Johan,' Emma ordered as they rounded a bend. The Rolls slid to a noiseless halt and she turned once more and said simply, 'The homestead.'

Teri gasped on an indrawn breath of wonder, and knew she would always remember her first view of Vins Doux. Impressive as the photos had been, they had not prepared her for the sheer beauty and grandeur that was Vins Doux. She had never seen a house quite like the one that was set against the shimmering mountains. The walls were white, a pristine white white that might have jarred on the eye had it not been relieved by the brown slatted shutters around the windows, and the shrubs that grew everywhere. The most striking feature was a gable, exquisitely curved. From her work in the library Teri knew enough about Cape Dutch architecture to recognise that this house had been designed by a master.

'It's the most beautiful house I've seen,' she said at last.

'It *is* beautiful, thank you.'

As the car moved on, Mrs Roland turned her head forward once more, but not before Teri glimpsed the look of sadness in her eyes. What did Vins Doux mean to her? If the wine estate was indeed her home, how could she have endured to leave it? And what had prompted her return?

CHAPTER TWO

QUESTIONS bubbled on Teri's lips, but it was more than the chauffeur's rigid back which deterred her from giving them voice. Emma Roland was a woman of mystery. There must be a reason why she had chosen to live in a small Johannesburg flat, content with just a few friends and the simplest of clothes. The suit she wore now was simple too, but it was well cut and expensive, and for the first time since Teri had known her, her hair had been styled by a good hairdresser. Her image today was one of unaffected elegance. It was an image that was new to Teri.

If the air of mystery was new, the aura of privacy was not. From the beginning Teri had known Emma Roland to be a private person; warm and friendly, her face radiating kindness even when it was in repose, yet private nevertheless. Teri remembered no shared confidences, no tales of the past.

It was a privacy that she knew she must respect. Emma would speak when she was ready to.

They drew up before the house and the chauffeur walked around the car to open the door for Emma Roland, then for Teri. 'Thank you, Johan,' Emma said, and then, 'Come, my dears, I think we are expected.'

An understatement. No sooner had they reached the foot of the wide steps leading up to the house than the big wooden door opened and the staff poured out. Wide smiles showed evident happiness at Emma Roland's return. She greeted each one in turn, pausing to ask after their families. One woman received a warm hug. 'Esther, our housekeeper here for more than twenty years,' Emma explained to Teri, before introducing the two newcomers. 'This is Miss Malloy, and the pretty little girl is Jill. Teri, my dear, I think we'll go inside now.'

A few paces took them into a hall that was spacious and gleaming, with a floor of polished oak and panelled walls, and a lovely antique chest in one corner. On the chest was a Chinese vase filled with roses from the garden. Teri would have liked to look around her, in particular to see the living room that led off from the hall, and which she could just glimpse a small part of through the open door, but Emma seemed in no mood to linger.

Holding Jill by the hand, Teri followed her friend into a carpeted corridor. 'This way takes us to the bedroom wing,' said Emma, and as she turned Teri saw that her face was suddenly very tired.

'You should rest,' she suggested with quick concern.

'I'll do just that.' Emma smiled down at Jill. 'This little mite is nearly asleep on her feet. Why don't you put her down and then do some exploring on your own.'

The very thing that Teri had in mind.

With delight she took in the two adjoining rooms that would be Jill's and her own. The walls were a pale primrose, and the colour was repeated in the curtains and bedspreads and the soft thick carpet which also contained splashes of jade. As in the entrance hall, the furniture was antique, lovely pieces, not very different from some that Teri had seen featured in books on Cape Dutch furniture. She would enjoy studying them, she knew, but not now.

'Bed for you,' she told Jill, and the little girl, sleepy eyes widening with amazement, pointed to a big four poster and echoed, 'Bed?'

In no time Jill was asleep. Teri stood and watched her a few minutes. Long lashes cast dusty shadows on a face that was far too pale. It would take time for Jill to build up her strength, but do so she would. Teri thought of the lovely garden she had glimpsed on her way into the house, of lonely inlets and sunny beaches, and she knew that she had been right to accept Mrs Roland's invitation.

It did not take long to unpack, and she was relieved to find the new clothes had travelled well. Here and there were a few creases, but she could iron them out later. Now, with the sweet-smelling air seducing her through the open window, she wanted only to be out of doors.

Her inclination was to pull on a pair of fading jeans and a shirt which she had owned before, and in which she felt most comfortable, but just half an hour at Vins Doux had made her realise that something else would be expected of Mrs Roland's companion. She stood before the open wardrobe, and her sense of wonder was akin to the emotions she had experienced when she had made her purchases. So many pretty clothes, and all of them belonging to Jill and herself. She had a faint inkling of how Cinderella must have felt before the bells had chimed midnight.

After a shower in a bathroom that was as tasteful as the bedrooms, she chose a flared skirt of powder blue, teaming it with a matching shirt in a lovely soft silk. She ran a brush through honey-coloured hair and applied just a little make-up to a face that glowed with excitement so that it needed no artificial enhancement. Then she went into the interleading room where Jill lay sleeping, one arm around her beloved teddy-bear. The little girl's breathing was slow and regular; she would sleep for some time and it was safe to leave her.

It was very hot in the garden, and the air was heavy

with the scent of roses and the drone of bees. Near the
path was a water-sprinkler, the drops falling on the
concrete, and Teri lingered a few moments to enjoy
the coolness of the spray on her hot cheeks. She
walked on, turning now and then to look at the house.
The path twisted and turned, and from every aspect
the house looked slightly different, but always it was
perfection. Teri wondered anew how Emma Roland
could have left it.

The path began to slope upwards. At the top of a
rise Teri stopped and sucked in her breath. She was
just yards from the vineyards. Sloping away, almost
from the point where she stood, they stretched before
her, to all sides of her. Waves of green and purple
rolled and rippled in the breeze, a vista that ended
only where it reached the blue-shadowed mountains.
Teri thought she had never seen anything quite so
beautiful.

She began to walk once more, a spring in her step.
She would come here with Jill. She would lift her little
sister in her arms so that she could touch the grapes
that hung in swollen bunches from the vines. When
Emma's foot was quite recovered they would all come
here together.

At a little clearing she stopped. The grass was cut
short here, and a smooth rock was invitingly shaped to
support a weary back. Not that she was weary, just
pleasantly drowsy after all the excitement. She sat
down on the ground and leaned back, and looked at
the mountains. Her eyes felt heavy, and she thought
she would close them just for a moment, no longer
than that, for soon it would be time to go back and
there was still so much that she wanted to see.

She did not know that she had fallen asleep until a
hand touched her arm and a voice said, 'There are
snakes here.'

She woke instantly, but she kept her eyes closed. The words were shocking enough. But the voice—she had heard that voice in her dreams! Slowly, very slowly, she let her lashes rise and she looked up.

'You!' They both said it at once, and the surprise was common and instantaneous.

He recovered first. He had straightened after touching her, and now he stood looking down at her. Sloan Garfield at his most imperious.

'I don't believe you—about the snakes, I mean.' Teri didn't know what made her say it, except that at that moment there seemed nothing else to say, and it seemed important to speak, if only to hide her shock.

'A mamba was killed here just a few days ago.'

In an instant she was on her feet. 'In this gorgeous spot?'

'Serpent in paradise,' he said mockingly. 'Snakes love that warm rock, that's why we keep the undergrowth around it cut short.'

We? Teri looked at him and felt something turn over inside her. The strangest feeling, she had never experienced anything remotely like it before. We? Mrs Roland had denied that Sloan Garfield had had anything to do with her decision to return to Vins Doux. Had Teri guessed that he would be here she would never have agreed to come.

And that was not altogether true. She thought now that somehow, without ever admitting it to herself consciously, she had known all along.

Serpent in paradise. Was he the serpent in paradise? Sloan Garfield, tall and tough and hard, and yes, devastatingly handsome if you liked that brand of uncompromisingly male good looks, which she did not, Teri decided very firmly. Vins Doux was as close to paradise as any place could be, and now Sloan had materialised to ruin it for her.

'We?' she asked, infusing her voice with all the coldness she could summon. 'You had a hand in killing the mamba?'

'One of the men helped me.' His eyes were very blue, and as penetrating as if he could see right through her to her innermost thoughts—which he could *not*.

'You work here, then?' She was pandering to him with her curiosity, and yet she could not seem to help herself.

There was just the briefest of pauses before he said, 'I see to things, yes.'

She recalled the first time she had met him. Wearing a suit that proclaimed elegance and taste in every well-cut inch, he had had the look of a business-man, a highly successful one at that. Now, with the sun gilding the thick fair hair as he towered above her, the image he presented was very different. In denims and a shirt that revealed tanned throat and arms, he looked like a man who spent his days out of doors.

And yet in some ways he had not changed at all. There was the look of power she had noticed the first time; the same blend of arrogance and sensuousness. And, no denying it, a sexuality which had made her think, perhaps consciously for the first time, of a passion that might exist in herself.

A hand reached down to her, and involuntarily she flinched.

'Do you always react so strongly?' His voice was sardonic. 'I was only going to help you up.'

The idea of grasping that big male hand was oddly disturbing, but he would think it strange if she refused the gesture. Though she could have stood up perfectly well by herself she took the proffered hand, noting abstractedly that the fingers beneath their coating of fine earth were long and well shaped. It was an impression that fled her mind as a tingling flamed up her wrist and her arm. The moment she was upright she took a step away from him and withdrew her own hand. Behaviour that was natural enough, but she saw that his eyes glinted.

'You haven't told me what you're doing here, Miss Malloy.'

She stared at him. If his position at Vins Doux were of any importance, surely Emma would have told him. 'I'm Mrs Roland's companion.'

'Ah!' Blue eyes and a long jaw went suddenly hard. His gaze had been on her face. Now it moved downwards, deliberately, to linger on her body. Teri held her breath as anger rose inside her. When the probing eyes lifted once more she was ready for him.

'Scrutiny complete?'

'Thank you, yes.'

The gall of the man, to sound quite so self-assured! At the least he could have apologised for his appalling manners.

'I'm so glad.'

Disdainfully she lifted her head, and walked away from him. Only a step or two, for then a hand took her wrist. Teri forced herself to stand very still.

'When did this come to pass?' he asked, before she could speak.

Something dangerous in his voice, even more than the strangeness of the question, had her swinging round to stare at him.

'What do you mean?'

'You were Emma Roland's companion in Johannesburg?'

'Of course not, you must know that.' She broke off. Evidently he knew even less than she thought. 'My job began today, here, at Vins Doux.'

'I see.'

It must be an overworked imagination that endowed

his tone with menace.

'Let go my arm,' she ordered.

'You're going back to the house?'

'Yes.' Long fingers played on the sleeve of her shirt burning through the fabric and on to her arm. Teri said, 'Was there something else you wanted to say, Mr Garfield?'

'Just a compliment. What a nice outfit you're wearing, Miss Malloy.'

The last thing she would have expected from him. About to say a mechanical thank you, Teri checked herself just in time. For the compliment was not well meant at all. She had only to look at the mirthless smile to know that.

Without a word she turned away, quickly this time, giving him no chance to see the confusion in her face or to detain her again.

Back she went, through the vineyards and the garden. The homestead was in view now, beautiful, architecturally perfect. Serpent in paradise—Sloan's words came back to Teri. If Vins Doux was indeed a kind of paradise, she could only hope that Sloan Garfield was not the serpent who would destroy her happiness in it.

Jill was still asleep when Teri returned, but she must have been ready to wake, for at the sound of the door she stirred. The little face, rosy with sleep, creased in a drowsy smile and two arms, painfully thin, wound themselves about Teri's neck.

'Ready to get up, Jilly?' Teri lifted the child from her bed, and carried her to a chair by the window. Hugging the small warm body to her, she looked outside. The rose-garden was below her, and Esther, the housekeeper, was cutting roses, filling a basket with the blooms.

The photographs of Vins Doux had indeed not done justice to the estate. It was more beautiful than anything Teri had imagined, and she knew quite certainly that her sister could not fail to thrive here.

Wispy hair was soft against her cheek, and suddenly Teri buried her face in it. She had done the right thing in coming to Vins Doux. She must not forget it. She must not let Sloan Garfield allow her to forget it. He meant nothing to her, and he could disturb her only if she chose to let him do so.

It was strange that Emma Roland hadn't mentioned that he would be here. But perhaps it wasn't strange at all. There were also other things of which she had not spoken. And there was no reason, really, why she should have singled out one member of her staff.

That was the strangest thing of all—Sloan Garfield did not have the look of being anything but his own man.

She gave her head a violent shake, causing Jill to look up puzzled. 'It's nothing, poppet.' Teri pressed the little head back against her chest. There was no way she could explain to the child her exasperation at the fact that the man she had decided not to think about was so hard to push from her mind. She could not even explain to herself why this should be so.

Glancing at her watch, Teri saw that it was nearly dinner-time. Of Emma Roland there had been no sign. She had looked so tired, perhaps she was still sleeping. There were things Teri would have liked to ask. Should she dress up for dinner? Was she likely to run often into Sloan Garfield. . . .

Heavens! she was at it again, and after she had decided not to give him a moment's thought. It was up to her to avoid Sloan, and it could not be too hard to do so. Vins Doux was a huge estate, and her duties and Sloan's ran in different directions. She would be with Emma in the house or in the garden. Sloan would be busy in the vineyards. Their paths would not cross. At least not often.

As for the question of dressing up, Teri was not yet aware of the customs at Vins Doux. Tonight or tomorrow Mrs Roland would tell her the things she had to know. In the meantime she could only use her own discretion.

Jill was pirouetting from one room to the other, a two-year-old female excited with the delights of a pretty new dress. A twirling butterfly, enchanting in her raiment of lace-edged pink. Smiling, Teri watched her a few moments, and suffered a pang of sorrow for the parents who would never see an adorable baby grow into a lovely girl.

The smile was replaced by a frown as she turned to her wardrobe. The choice should have been so simple; oddly it wasn't simple at all.

Fifteen minutes later she studied herself in the mirror. 'This dress does things for you,' the saleslady had enthused at the time of the purchase, and Teri knew that the words had been more than just sales pitch. A subtle blending of emerald and turquoise enhanced her delicate colouring, adding lustre to green eyes and to cheeks that had been warmed by the afternoon in the sun. It was a simple dress, but its expense was evident in its elegant lines. The snug bodice hinted sensuously at shapely breasts, the skirt was graceful over slim hips and revealed long legs to their best advantage.

Normally not given to spending much time on her appearance, Teri wondered why she did so now. Leaning forward, she applied a touch of green eye-shadow and some dark mascara. All at once the elfin-shaped face was all eyes. The effect was startling.

Did a quiet dinner at home necessitate so much

preparation? Yes, Teri told herself, this was Emma Roland's first evening back home, and she would appreciate the effort to make it special. And then Teri gave a small sharp exclamation of anger. Who was she trying to fool? At least with herself she could be honest. The effort was for a man she didn't like and who made no effort to conceal the fact that he did not like her. A man who would not even be present tonight.

But he was there. She saw him the moment she came into the dining-room. Her breath jerked, and she gripped Jill's hand tightly, as if to draw strength from the little girl at her side.

Sloan had his back to her. He was talking to Mrs Roland at the far end of the room. By the time they registered her presence and turned, Teri's breathing had returned to normal and she was able to smile.

'I'm glad to see you looking so rested,' she said to Emma, ignoring the man at her side.

'Oh, I feel much better. Plane journeys drain me every time, but three hours of shameless sleeping have restored me. Sloan, you've already met my companion. And this beguiling child,' she bent and drew Jill forward, 'is little Jill Malloy.'

Teri had been watching Emma's pleasure in the little girl. Now some instinct brought her up to face Sloan Garfied. Contempt, more chilling than anything she had yet seen, had spread over the lean features. The blue eyes bore a hardness she was beginning to recognise, the long jaw was a steel line.

Teri stared at him, momentarily confused, and felt her heart pounding.

'I didn't know you had a child, Miss Malloy.' The emphasis was on the word 'Miss'.

The confusion was gone. 'You're judging me,' Teri thought as anger rose inside her. 'You think Jill is my daughter, and you're presuming to judge me.'

Chin lifting in a manner which Louise would have recognised as heralding battle, she replied sweetly, 'There are things you don't know about me, Mr Garfield.'

Beside her she heard Emma draw breath. For a few moments she had actually forgotten the woman's presence. In those moments it had seemed as if there were only two people in the room, Teri Malloy and Sloan Garfield, battle lines defined sharply between them. Emma opened her mouth, as if to speak. 'Jill is Teri's sister,' she would say, just as if Sloan needed an explanation, not understanding that he did not deserve it.

Teri threw her a quick look of appeal. Don't explain, please don't explain. Would Emma understand? No . . . the kind elderly face was puzzled. And then, incredibly, yes! She did understand, for a shimmer of mischief appeared in her eyes.

Calmly, as if the words had been the ones she'd intended all along, Emma said, 'Sloan and I have already helped ourselves to drinks. What will you have, Teri dear?'

Looking at the array of bottles, Teri wondered what she should choose. Her acquaintance with alcohol was limited to the very occasional bottle of wine she and Andy had shared over a meal. About to ask Emma what she would recommend, she heard an insolent voice ask, 'A lemonade, Miss Malloy?'

'Perfect,' she replied sweetly, 'for Jill.' And when the little girl had been given her glass, she said, 'A whisky for me, I think.'

'With soda?'

'On the rocks,' Teri told him provocatively, repeating a phrase she had read often enough.

'On the rocks?' Mrs Roland echoed incredulously, and Teri knew that she had surprised her again; until that moment she had always stuck to orange juice, even when Emma was having her after-dinner sherry. 'Might be reckless on an empty stomach,' the older woman demurred.

'Oh, I think not,' said Sloan, sensuous lips curling in a wicked taunt. 'Miss Malloy has a penchant for recklessness.'

'How could you know?' Emma was curious. 'This is just the second time that you two have met.'

'Third,' said Teri, realising that Emma did not know of the afternoon's encounter. She looked at Sloan, taking in the ruggedly handsome features. Hating him.

There was no chance to explain, for Sloan was handing her a glass. As she took it from him his fingers made contact with hers. A deliberate contact, she realised, when the fingers remained on the glass after they could have released it. She could have moved her own fingers, she supposed afterwards, and wondered why she hadn't.

Mercifully, the long fingers lifted at length, breaking contact. The whole incident had lasted no more than seconds. It made no sense that Teri should feel dizzy.

Sloan was still close to her, his head inclined, and she heard him murmur softly, 'Fourth time, actually,' and then he had moved away, and was lifting his own glass to his lips.

She looked at him again, without meaning to, and found him waiting for her. Four times. . . . Perhaps it was strain that had made her forget the first meeting, when she had thrown mud at his car. But Sloan had not forgotten. He was a man who would not forget things. She suppressed a shiver.

'Miss Malloy seems to like rocks,' he observed mildly.

'Teri—Sloan. First names, please. Teri would prefer it that way, I'm sure—wouldn't you dear?—and you've never been one to stand on ceremony, Sloan.' Emma looked from one to the other. 'And now do tell me about this third meeting. Rocks and recklessness— I'm intrigued!'

'We met this afternoon. I had to wake Teri.' Her name sounded odd on his lips, she could not have said why. 'She was sleeping against the big rock near the west vineyard.'

'In the clearing?' Emma asked in consternation. 'We've had snakes there. Oh lord, Teri, I never thought to warn you!'

'You couldn't have known I'd wander that way.' The girl kept her voice light.

'Yes, but still. . . . Just as well you spotted her, Sloan.'

'Just as well,' he agreed. 'We killed a mamba there only last week.' And then, oh so politely, 'You're not drinking your whisky, Teri?'

'Cheers.'

She lifted her glass to her lips. Only supreme effort stopped a gasp as liquid fire attacked her throat. Quickly dropping her eyes, she let her lashes conceal her shock.

'You don't have to drink it,' a low male voice informed her.

A moment was all she needed to regain some semblance of control. Lifting her head, she met the blue-eyed gaze squarely. 'I drink this all the time.'

Deliberately she took another sip, keeping her eyes on his, and this time she was ready for the fire of the alcohol, and she did not flinch.

'Hm,' said Sloan. Just one syllable, and Teri wished she knew what he meant by it. His eyes glinted with something that looked very much like amusement. She hated him even more. Words bubbled on her lips, there were things she wanted to tell him. And then on the periphery of her vision she registered Emma Roland—for a few moments she had been unaware once more of her employer's existence—and she thought better of it.

'I think,' said Sloan, addressing Emma, 'that Teri should be told a few facts before she wanders out on her own again.'

'Right.' Emma looked worried. 'Like any big place Vins Doux does have its dangers.'

Other rocks where snakes liked to hide? A beach, perhaps, where the tide came in quickly so that the unwary sunbather could be cut off by water?

'For Jill's sake it would be best if I was forewarned.' Teri smiled, but she felt anything but amused, for instinct told her that the worst danger, the danger to *herself*, did not lie in snakes or tides, but in a totally different quarter.

'Hungry,' a small voice piped.

'We're about to eat, darling,' Mrs Roland told Jill as she led the way to the table and summoned a servant with a brief shake of a silver bell. 'Why don't we all sit down?'

The meal was not sumptuous, but in the gracious dining-room it gave the impression of being so. Table and chairs were of walnut, the rich polished sheen set off perfectly against curtains and carpet of dark gold. The cutlery was a heavy Cape Dutch silver, the porcelain so delicate that Teri gave a mental cross to her fingers in the hope that Jill would not break or chip a plate.

There was lamb, delicately flavoured, and served with new potatoes and tiny peas and a crisp salad. And there was wine. Emma lifted a fine crystal glass to her lips, took a sip, then smiled across at Sloan. 'Perfect,' she pronounced. 'And if I'm not wrong I think I recognise the vintage.'

'You're not wrong,' he smiled back at her, and his eyes had in them none of the hardness Teri had observed in her own encounters with him.

'Vins Doux wine?' she asked.

She saw Mrs Roland field a brief glance from Sloan before she answered. 'Not in this instance. This wine was bottled at a neighbouring estate called Bienvenue, and Sloan knows it's a favourite of mine.'

The wine was delicious, sparkling and light, yet not too sweet, making Teri feel pleasantly languorous. Emma was talking to Sloan, wine business which Teri did not understand, and as her earlier tension drained away she began to enjoy the meal and let the conversation wash over her.

She was glad she had changed her clothes, for the dress struck just the right note of casual elegance she saw everywhere around her. Mrs Roland wore a simple two-piece jersey suit in dove-grey, beautifully cut, with a slim choker of pearls at the neck as her only adornment. Sloan had on well-fitting navy trousers with a silk shirt of a lighter blue that almost matched his eyes. The shirt was open at the neck, revealing the thrust of his throat. His hair was slightly damp, as if he had recently showered, and in the soft light of the table candelabrum his face was mellowed. So engrossed was he in his conversation with Emma that it was safe to look at him.

He looked totally at home, Teri thought. A man in command of his surroundings, and at ease with himself. No stranger seeing the two at the table would realise that an employer was being briefed by a member of her staff on events that had taken place in her absence.

Sloan turned his head quite suddenly, giving Teri

no time to hide her eyes. He knows I've been staring at him, she thought, cconfused, and to her horror she felt a flush warm her cheeks. Damn the man, even the softening influence of the candlelight did not lessen an attractiveness that was at once devilish and dynamic.

The effect he had on women must do marvels for his ego. Pity the poor woman who would choose to live with him, he must be insufferable. Was he married? She didn't know, and didn't want to know, she told herself crossly, wondering why on earth such a question had even entered her mind.

CHAPTER THREE

'WE must be boring you, Teri,' said Sloan.

'Not at all,' she smiled at him, determinedly meeting his eyes.

'Know something about wine-making?'

Testing me, are you? Her smile deepened disarmingly. 'I know very little, but I'm enormously interested. I plan to learn a lot more about wine.'

'I'm glad.' Emma sounded oddly pleased.

In Sloan's autocratic face there was no similar sign of joy. The sensuous lips tightened as the eyes assumed an expression that was little short of forbidding.

You don't want me here, Teri thought. There's more to this than just a natural antipathy. You don't like me, you don't want me, and I wish I knew why.

'Seems you chose the right person to come here with you, Emma,' she heard Sloan say.

Emma. Teri hoped that her own face did not mirror her surprise. The ease with which Sloan called his employer Emma suggested an intimacy that she had not expected. Until now she had thought she would be able to avoid him; had assumed that he was present here tonight only because it was Mrs Roland's first day home and there was much to discuss. It was disconcerting to realise that there was a friendly relationship between these two, and that as a result she might be forced to see Sloan more often than she had reckoned with.

'I know I chose the right person.' Dimly she registered Emma's response.

'You didn't mention a companion.'

Mrs Roland would reprimand him. Gracious lady that she was, she would nevertheless refuse to allow an employee to question her in such an insolent manner. For it was insolent, Teri thought, even though the tone of the words had been friendly enough.

'Ah, Sloan, I echo Teri's earlier comment. There are things you don't know about *me* either.' Emma was laughing, and the glimmer of mischief Teri had glimpsed in her eyes at the start of the evening was in evidence again.

'You intrigue me.' An answering smile curved the corners of strong lips, but the blue eyes were hooded.

'Marvellous! You shouldn't mind, Sloan. You like pretty women, and you must admit my companion is lovely.'

Teri forced herself to sit very still as Sloan's gaze returned to her, as it moved deliberately from her eyes to her mouth, lingering there for a moment before it moved downwards to where her breasts were a soft swell beneath the figure-hugging dress.

'Lovely indeed,' he drawled.

As before, on the surface a compliment, yet not a compliment at all. The blatant gaze infuriated her, and at the same time left her oddly shaken. Only Mrs Roland's presence at the table prevented her from lashing out with a furious retort.

His eyes remained steady, they did not lift back to her face. For the second time that day Teri had the strangest feeling. Admiration from a male was nothing new, and at twenty-two she knew why. Beautiful as an angel, Andy had called her, but he had put her on a pedestal. Honey-coloured hair and slanting green eyes, combined with a body that was slender yet curvaceous, had drawn more earthy comments from other men. Teri had learned to fend off unwanted passes, to lighten a heavy moment with a joke.

Though she felt sure that Sloan was undressing her mentally, his scrutiny was different from anything she had ever experienced. It was almost as if he was studying her dress, and not just the body it clothed. And that was ridiculous, she thought, and wished her heart would stop thudding against her ribs.

The plate fell suddenly. Jill must have tried a little too hard to push a piece of lamb on to her spoon, and the plate slid past her and on to the ground.

'Oh dear!' Teri was out of her chair in a moment, and kneeling on the carpet.

'Let it be,' she heard Emma's reassuring voice, but she did not heed it as she went on picking up fallen bits of food. She regretted the accident, yet she could not help being glad of the chance it gave her to conceal her confusion at Sloan's manner. By the time she had straightened she had regained her composure.

'I'm sorry about this.' Though Teri's eyes were solely on Emma, she was acutely aware of the silent man watching her.

'Not your fault, Teri, Jill's a baby.'

'She is, and she should really be eating off plastic plates. It's what she's used to. From now on it would be best.'

'I'm not sure we have any,' Emma said doubtfully, and Teri suppressed a smile of amusement. In the little Johannesburg flat, Mrs Roland had led the life of an ordinary mortal, but Vins Doux had the look of a place on which the invention of plastic had yet to make its mark.

'Could I get some? Cape Town's a little far, I know, but perhaps there's something nearer.'

'I'll ask Johan to pick something up for you,' Emma offered.

'No need for that,' Sloan interposed. 'Teri's

probably the best judge of what she needs, and as I'm
driving into the city tomorrow morning she might as
well come along.'

The words were addressed to Emma. Almost as if
she herself were invisible, Teri thought. She opened
her mouth to say no, only to check the refusal. She
was overreacting, and she knew why. The thought of
being in Sloan's company, alone, was unnerving. But
she could not let him know it, so she quietly said,
'That may be a good idea.'

'We'll leave here around nine.' With the matter
disposed of, Sloan seemed to forget her as he reverted
to the subject of the export market for wines. Which
suited her, Teri decided firmly. She would go with
him tomorrow, she could hardly do otherwise without
making herself look foolish. But the less contact she
had with the too self-assured Mr Sloan Garfield in the
future, the better.

Dinner was over, and they were in the living-room
drinking coffee, when Sloan glanced at his watch.

'You're going already?' Emma asked.

'I'm afraid so.' He frowned. 'I'm sorry to cut things
short like this your first evening back, Emma, but I'd
bought tickets for a show before I knew the date of
your return.'

'Don't be sorry. Going with anyone I know?'

His face was impassive. 'Miranda Hanson.'

'Of course.' Emma's voice was light. 'It's still quite
early, Sloan. Why not stay just a little longer?'

'I'd like that, but there's something I must still see to.
As it is, I just have time to get back to my—quarters.'

There seemed to be a slight emphasis on the last
word, but Teri had no time to ponder the significance
of that, for Emma said, 'Then we must certainly not
keep you,' and in her voice there was the suggestion of
laughter.

The door closed behind the tall figure of the man, and Teri felt her stomach muscles relax. Till this moment she had not realised quite how tense she had been.

From a velvet-covered armchair came a sigh; Jill had fallen asleep while the adults were talking. Remorsefully Teri went over to the sleeping child. Looking down at her, she wondered how Sloan's presence could have affected her to the exclusion of anything else.

'Poor mite,' came Emma's comment from behind her. 'She's had a long day.'

'And it's way past her bedtime. I think I'll take her to her room.'

'Will you wake her?' There was compassion in the older woman's eyes.

'No, I'll carry her, and put her into her bed just as she is. I won't even try to brush her teeth, she'd be very tearful if I did, and it won't matter if she sleeps in her clothes for once.'

'Come back when Jill is settled, and we'll have another cup of coffee.'

Teri smiled from the doorway, the sleeping child in her arms. 'I'd like that.'

Jill didn't wake, as her sister had known she wouldn't. In the huge primrose-quilted bed, with her beloved teddy by her side, the little girl looked even smaller than usual, and very vulnerable. Heart going out to her, Teri bent and gently stroked a strand of damp hair from her forehead before kissing it. 'Be happy at Vins Doux,' she whispered.

Returning to the living-room, she found Emma Roland leaning back in a chair, eyes closed. At the sound of Teri's footsteps she opened them.

'Past your own bedtime, I think,' Teri smiled.

'Just napping. It's been a long day for me too, but I

couldn't go to bed yet.' Emma poured coffee and handed a cup to Teri. 'Tell me what you think of Vins Doux.'

'It's wonderful, beyond anything I expected.' Teri could have elaborated, but there were other things on her mind. She looked directly into eyes that were warm and grey, and waiting for her. 'You didn't tell me Sloan would be here.'

'No.'

'I asked you about him.'

'You asked if he had something to do with my decision to go home, and I told you the decision was my own.'

'That's right.' Teri felt uncertain, but she stood her ground notwithstanding. 'You didn't mention that he would be here. And he obviously didn't know I was coming. Why didn't you say something, Mrs Roland?'

'Emma, please. Sloan calls me that, I think you should too.'

'Emma.' Teri tested the word on her tongue and was glad that the other woman had found a way of telling her that if she was now her employer she was nevertheless still her friend. 'Thank you, Emma. About Sloan. . . .'

'Would you have come if you'd known?'

'No!' emphatically.

A soft laugh. 'I wanted you to come. I was taking no chances.'

Teri could not help a laugh of her own. 'I've said before that you're a woman of guile.'

'Not of the malicious kind, I hope. Tell me, Teri, why do the sparks fly between you and Sloan?'

'You noticed. . . .'

'I may be getting on, but I'm not blind, dear, and there are certain things I remember very well from my own youth.'

Do you know what it's like to feel that every one of your nerves is tingling? That the air can be so electric that you sense you could touch it? Do you know what it's like to be alive to a man's sexuality and yet feel that you never want to see him again?

Tautly Teri stared at Emma. 'There seems to be a personality clash,' she agreed.

'What happened this afternoon?'

'Sloan found me sleeping against the rock. He woke me and put the fear of God in me.'

'Just as well. I should have warned you myself. That was all, Teri?'

Teri was silent as she gazed into the fireplace where a fire had been lit, and thought of the undercurrents in the afternoon's interchange.

Emma spoke into the silence. 'Sparks then too?'

'In a way, yes.'

'I don't understand why. It was only your second meeting, and in my flat you said barely three words to each other.'

Teri looked up with a wry grin. 'We'd met before.'

'Really!'

'On my way to you that day. I threw mud at Sloan's car.'

Emma's eyes were wide with delighted disbelief. 'Teri, you couldn't have!'

'I did.'

As Teri recounted the incident Emma began to laugh. She was still laughing when Teri fell silent. At last Emma wiped the tears from her eyes.

'Something new for Sloan,' she said when she could talk. 'Not one of his other women would dream of meting out such treatment. On the contrary, they tend to do the Walter Raleigh act with him—they'd cheerfully prostrate themselves on the ground and let him step over them if that would give them the attention they wanted.'

'They must be a bunch of idiots,' Teri said stiffly. 'And I'm not one of Sloan's women.'

'You're not,' Emma agreed.

'I'm afraid what happened has tainted me for ever in his eyes.'

'I don't believe it. Sloan's sense of humour has never let him down yet,' Emma said briskly.

'If he saw a funny side to what happened, he certainly hasn't let me know it.'

'Hm.' Emma looked thoughtful. 'Why did you let him think Jill was your child?'

'Because of his reaction.' Just the memory of that reaction, the chill in Sloan's voice when he'd said, 'I didn't know you had a child, Miss Malloy,' with that hateful emphasis on the word 'miss', made her angry again now.

'He drew his conclusions, I admit, but they were natural in the circumstances,' Emma pointed out.

'I've no argument with *that*.' Green eyes sparkled with a look that Emma Roland would come to know well. 'He judged me, Emma, and he had no right to do that.'

'Perhaps not. Will you tell him the truth when you see him tomorrow?'

'I might.' The look Teri cast Emma was so filled with unconscious pleading that the older woman thought few male hearts could have withstood it. 'If I don't, keep my secret, please, Emma.'

Grey eyes danced. 'I'm good at secrets.'

'I don't understand.'

'Of course not. Well, Teri dear, if you and Sloan decide to keep the sparks going between you, I can see that life at Vins Doux will be interesting.'

Honey-coloured hair bounced as Teri jerked up. 'I hope I won't have to see him often.'

'He's driving you into town tomorrow.'

'Other than that. . . . I'll be with you here in the house, or in the gardens, and Sloan spends his time in the vineyards. I gather he's some kind of foreman?'

'He—sees to things.'

'Almost the same words that Sloan had used.' It was time to divert the subject from Sloan Garfield. 'Emma, I was thinking, perhaps we could hook a wall-hanging?'

Emma's ready laugh sounded against the crackle of the fire. 'You'll be keeping me busy, child!'

'You're so good with your hands and they're fun to do.' Teri looked around doubtfully, sensing that a home-crafted piece would be out of place amidst the antique splendours of Vins Doux. 'On second thoughts, I suppose there'd be nowhere to hang it.'

'Jill's room could do with a pretty thing. A nursery scene perhaps,' Emma suggested. 'I think I'd enjoy rug-hooking. Why don't you get something when you're in town tomorrow?'

Before getting into bed that night Teri went into Jill's room. The little girl had moved in her sleep and the unaccustomed quilt had slid from her legs. As Teri covered her, she wondered how long it would take for Jill to grow used to the new room. Such a beautiful room it was, but an adults' room, not a nursery. A scene designed especially for children would make a big difference.

Emma's suggestion held a hint of permanence. A temporary kind of permanence anyway, if there was logic in such a thought. Teri and Jill would not live with Emma always, but several months would give some much-needed stability to Jill, and a breathing-space to her sister.

It was a thought that should bring happiness, and in fact it did bring relief. But there was also doubt. If only there was no Sloan Garfield at Vins Doux. No serpent in paradise. Perhaps he would leave, decide to

work elsewhere. And that was wishful thinking indeed,
Teri told herself as she slid between the sheets.

'Just going shopping,' Teri muttered crossly to herself
as she stood before the array of new clothes in the
wardrobe.

So why was she so indecisive? Jill was dressed and
ready and amusing herself by opening and closing the
drawers of an antique tallboy. And still Teri had not
decided what to wear.

The pink slack-suit was what she had had in mind.
Pretty, practical, it was the kind of outfit she would
have chosen to wear for a shopping trip with Andy.
But Sloan Garfield was not Andy.

A vision came into her mind. Sloan. Tall and
sinuous, altogether too good-looking for his own ego;
and for the peace of mind of any woman who found
herself in his company.

There was another vision. Miranda—the unseen
Miranda. She would be slim and elegant, sophisticated.

As she herself could be sophisticated, Teri decided.
Sophisticated in a manner befitting Mrs Roland's
companion. She would command Sloan's respect even
if she could not have his liking.

Making her choice with sudden decisiveness, she
reached for one of her new outfits. The dress, a
daringly attractive mix of red and orange, had narrow
shoulder straps and a wide belt. A white jacket went
over it and a chunky necklace fitted snugly around the
slender throat.

Time to turn her attention to her hair. Sloan had
only seen it worn down. On the infamous day of the
mud-slinging it had been caught back in a snood; since
her arrival at Vins Doux it had hung loose, swinging on
her shoulders in a silken honey swathe. Drawing it up
and back from her face, she coiled it in a chignon, with

just a few strands loose on either side to counter any
undue severity. Her make-up was equally deft—eyes
darkened and shaded, and a lipstick that went well
with the colours of the dress.

All that was left was to assume an appearance of
elegant poise. Lifting her head, Teri took Jill by the
hand and glided from the room, legs and hips and
shoulders moving in graceful unison.

Sloan was waiting for her at the foot of the wide
stone steps. He was leaning against the silver car she
had abused at their first meeting, his jacket slung
negligently over one shoulder. Legs, clad in immaculate brown trousers, were crossed one over the other.
A silk shirt of a slightly darker colour somehow
contrived to suggest the muscularity of broad chest
and shoulders.

His eyes were on her, steady, appraising, taking in
every detail of her own appearance. Teri took a deep
breath and gripped Jill's hand just a little more tightly
before making her way, as smoothly as she could,
down the steps.

Emma emerged from the house, and came smiling
down to the car to join them. 'How smart you both
look,' she enthused. 'Don't they look nice, Sloan?'

'Two females to do any man credit.' He was smiling
too, but his tone was dry.

'Thank you,' said Teri graciously, and wondered if
Sloan and Emma sensed that beneath her poised
exterior beat a heart as agitated as if it belonged to a
girl on her first date.

Sloan opened the car doors, seating Teri in the front
and Jill at the back, his manner so polite as to defy
faulting. Wildly Teri wondered if it was only her
imagination that made her pick up an inherent
mockery where none existed.

Slowly he negotiated the winding oak-lined drive of

Vins Doux, and then they passed through the gates and the car took the tarred highway with purring speed.

Teri turned her face to the window, staring out with fierce concentration. She had been this way just yesterday, but she was so disturbingly aware of the man at the wheel that it seemed necessary to look anywhere but in his direction.

'Enjoying the scenery?' His voice came to her as if from a distance.

'It's very beautiful.'

It *was* beautiful, at least she remembered it as being so. Lush vineyards. Misty mountains, standing a brooding sentinel over silent valleys. The sea, as deep a blue as if a thousand bottles of ink had been emptied in the water. She would come this way again, and she would enjoy the beauty to the fullest. But she could not enjoy it today, not with Sloan just inches away from her, with the air so sparked with tension that it was becoming increasingly hard to breathe.

She needed more air. Her hand went to the door, fumbled with a lever, but nothing happened.

'Want the window open?'

'Yes,' she said coolly, wishing she had not attempted the exercise; her vain attempts might affect her careful illusion of poise. 'What do I do?'

'This.' The car did not slacken its speed as Sloan reached past Teri. She made herself sit very still as his hand slid by her breast, arm resting hard against it as a finger touched a knob. The merest flick and the window edged electronically downward, the whole operation over in less than two seconds. But the arm took longer to move. For what seemed like eternity it rested against her breast. When it withdrew, there was a burning sensation where it had been.

Teri took a jerky breath. Sloan was whistling gently,

and involuntarily she turned from the window to look at him. By no outward sign did he show himself aware of her scrutiny. And that was just one more way in which he went out of his way to deliberately humiliate her.

'You did that purposely,' she accused, angry all at once.

'Of course.' Not even a pretence at embarrassment.

'And you thought I'd be too taken aback to react.'

'No mud available,' he countered mildly.

Horrible man, always so sarcastic. She was getting angrier every moment. 'I do have a hand,' she informed him.

'You'd hardly slap me and risk an accident—not with your daughter in the back seat.'

Daughter. Some time during the night she had decided to tell him the truth about Jill. To let him believe that Jill was anything but her sister seemed a childish charade—but in an instant she changed her mind. Sloan was so sure of himself, so totally sure of himself. There was some satisfaction in knowing that she had him fooled.

'I would do nothing to endanger Jill.' She paused, swept with pain at the memory of the parents who had died so needlessly. More quietly she added, 'But don't touch me again. I won't stand for it.'

There was little traffic on this stretch of road, and Sloan was able to move his eyes sidewards with safety.

'You're hardly untouched.' It was said dispassionately enough as his eyes, those eyes that were as blue as the Cape sea, lingered on her face.

'Touched but choosy,' Teri responded, deciding to treat the remark with the disdain it deserved.

'Prickly too. And unashamed.' He laughed. 'Look ahead, Teri, see that mill? It's one of the oldest hereabouts, a real landmark.'

An unexpected peace-offering. Why had this arrogant and disturbing man chosen to make it? Was Sloan calling an end to battle, or was this merely a truce? Only time would tell.

Nevertheless, it was with a lightening of the heart that Teri watched the approach into Cape Town. 'One of the loveliest cities in the world,' her mother had once told her, and though Teri's acquaintance with all the world was limited she did not think that the statement had been exaggerated. Set against Table Mountain, Cape Town was an awesome sight.

As they came into the city Teri sat forward in her seat, delighted with the sights all around her. Old houses with wrought-iron railed porches and complex gables. Narrow streets climbing torturously up the slope of the mountain. And then the foreshore, the Heerengracht, built on land that had been reclaimed from the sea, with buildings that were modern and beautiful. Teri did not know if Sloan was giving her a guided tour of the city—he did not say, and she would not ask—but she did know that she would come here again, alone, and that she would spend hours exploring.

'The Parade Ground,' said Sloan, as he turned into a big open ground in the centre of the city. On one side of it was an ancient castle, on another was the gracious building that constituted the city hall.

'This was the original military parade ground,' Sloan explained as he negotiated the car expertly into a space that looked too small for it. 'It's still used sometimes on formal occasions, but for the main part it's a car park. And on certain days'—he lifted his hand from the wheel in a gesture—'it's also used as a market.'

A superb market at that. Everywhere there were stalls. Some were piled high with fruit—peaches and

plums and mangoes and lichees in glorious profusion.
In others there were flowers; roses and dahlias, asters
and zinnias, in all colours. The salespeople were
mostly Malay women, handsome people dressed in
lovely sari-like garments, calling to each other in a
language that Teri did not understand.

Utterly enchanted, she took in the sounds, the
scents. It was all more colourful, more exotic, than
anything she had envisaged. She would have liked to
spend more time here, to go from one stall to another,
but Sloan was beside her, and Jill was tugging at her
hand, and regretfully she fell into step with them.

He left her in Adderley Street, outside a big
department store, and showed her the spot where they
would meet. 'Two hours enough time?' he asked her,
and she smiled her agreement, for the moment
forgetting the cool sophistication which did not come
naturally to her.

It was easy enough to find the department she
wanted. Plastic utensils were there in every shape and
colour, and Teri watched contentedly as Jill dithered
for ten minutes before deciding on red.

Next stop was the crafts section, and once again
Teri let her sister make a choice. It was not often that
the little girl was let loose in a shop, and once Teri had
decided which kind of wall-hanging to go for, it was a
question of choosing the actual picture. Jill agonised
between three angelic-faced kittens and a puppy with
huge liquid eyes. She could not decide, she just could
not decide. Eventually Teri gave in and bought both.
Emma wouldn't mind, she knew. Besides, this was a
case of two being better than one; instead of taking
turns with the hooking, she and Emma could work on
the hangings at the same time. More companionable
by far.

An hour had passed. It would not be difficult to

while away the other hour. There was so much to see in the store, so many lovely things to admire. Only time had kept Teri from indulging in window-shopping in the past, and time was one thing she had now. It did not matter that she did not have the money to buy the things she saw, looking, touching, admiring, was enough.

She stayed a while longer in the crafts section, which seemed to concentrate especially on weaving. There were woven hangings of every description, samples to whet the eyes of those whose hobby weaving was. When the rug-hooked hangings were finished Emma might like to try weaving. Browsing through the catalogues, Teri saw that the possibilities were endless.

Jill was growing restless when Teri realised it was time to move on. Next to the hardware section where they had arranged to meet Sloan was the toy department. As Jill's gaze fell upon a scene straight out of toyland, her eyes widened, and for a moment she stood quite rigid with astonishment. Then she let out a whoop of delight and grabbed a small rubber doll.

'Dolly! Jill have dolly?'

A mental picture of her near-empty wallet convinced Teri that her little sister could not have the doll. Her finances needed careful watching, even now, when they lived beneath a rent-free roof.

Regretfully she shook her head. 'Sorry, love.'

Jill looked mournful a moment, then brightened. There was so much to see, to touch, to explore. Clutching the rubber doll to her chest, she darted from one aisle to the next. Teri watched her, and wished that just for once she could indulge in a purchase of impulse. As dolls went this one was not expensive, and it would mean so much to Jill. For Christmas perhaps. . . .

The little girl was having the time of her life. She had found a rocking horse, and with the doll still in her arms she climbed on to it and began to rock. That it was the most exciting thing she had ever done was evidenced by her shrieks of delight and fear. To and fro she rocked, faster and faster.

Louise should see her like this, Teri thought. Excited, stimulated by the novelty of a strange toy, she was a different child from the one who had been pale and ill and too quiet for so much of the time. Soon the pale cheeks would have colour in them, they could hardly help growing rosy in the invigorating air of Vins Doux. Teri would take photos of her then, and she'd send a few to Louise.

From the clock department nearby came a sudden chiming. Teri glanced down at her own watch. Could two hours have passed so quickly? Sloan would be waiting for them, and he had the air of a man who liked to be punctual.

'Time to be going, love,' she told Jill as she lifted her from the horse. 'Give me the doll.'

'No.' The rubber doll was clutched tighter.

'Jill, darling, please. . . .'

'Want dolly!' It was a wail that grew higher and higher. 'Want dolly!'

'No, Jill.' Eyes were turning their way. Feeling like a child-abuser, Teri tried to take the doll away from Jill, but the little girl's grip was surprisingly tight. 'Want dolly!' she wailed again.

'When I have some money,' her sister conceded in despair. 'When I get paid. Oh, Jilly, please!'

'A determined little female,' an amused voice said from behind her, and Teri grew rigid.

Very slowly she turned. 'She's taken a fancy to the doll,' she said through stiff lips.

'So I gather. Are you going to buy it for her?'

'No.'

Sloan bent to look at the price-tag. 'It's not expensive.'

'More than I can afford, all the same.' Her throat was thick with distress. Why, oh, why hadn't he waited in the hardware department and spared her this humiliation?

Almost in self-defence, Teri said, 'I may buy it when I get paid at the end of the month.'

'If it's still available.' Sloan's tone was devoid of expression. 'How about something to eat before we start back?'

It was not a question, not really, for he seemed to take it for granted that she would say yes. She was thirsty, and yet as always there seemed the need to defy this man.

'I don't think so, but thanks anyway.'

'I imagine Jill wouldn't say no to an ice-cream.'

He was shrewd—which came as no surprise. The words might have been addressed to Teri, the tone, the eyes, were directed solely at her sister, and at the word 'ice-cream' the little girl's face shone with excitement. Teri knew that it was useless to argue— the issue had already been settled.

She decided to meet him halfway. 'A cup of tea would be nice, I suppose.'

'There's a pleasant place on the next block,' Sloan said. And then, 'Why don't you make your way over to that exit there? I'll catch up with you.'

The coffee-shop was more than pleasant. Teri looked around, enchanted despite the fact that she knew Sloan had used Jill as his means of bringing them in here. Decorated mainly in yellow—yellow checked cloths and sun-filter curtains of a slightly deeper shade, pictures of yellow flowers in yellow frames—the place was bright, the aura it projected friendly.

Teri was still marvelling at the effect colour could have on one's mood, when the words 'For you, Jill,' pulled her attention back to the table.

A package lay in front of the little girl. Even as Jill studied it mystified—it would take her a few moments before she decided to open it—Teri knew what was inside.

CHAPTER FOUR

TERI jerked around to look at Sloan, who was pulling out a chair for himself. As he sat down he met her gaze, and she saw that the corners of his lips were lifted slightly, and that the blue eyes held an expression which she did not understand.

Her chest felt tight. 'You bought the doll, didn't you?' She spoke quietly, so that Jill would not hear.

Sloan shrugged.

'You shouldn't have.' Teri's lips were stiff as Jill began to tear open the package.

'The child seemed to want it.'

And it cost little enough, his tone seemed to say.

Little enough in your frame of reference, Teri thought resentfully. A lot in mine.

It was hard to feel appreciative when her whole body quivered with strain. Had Andy bought the doll, she would have been grateful. But Sloan was not Andy—how often had she made the comparison, one that seemed strangely unfair to Andy each time.

Had Sloan made the gesture to annoy her? Yes, said the voice of intuition. And then again, perhaps not, she reasoned more charitably. They had got off to a bad start, she and Sloan. Perhaps he was trying to make amends. If that was unlikely, so many other unlikely things had occurred in the last weeks. Perhaps, after all, she should give him the benefit of the doubt.

She managed a smile. 'Jill does seem thrilled.'

Rubber toes now peeped through a tear in the paper, revealing to Jill the nature of the present.

58

Impatiently she tore open the rest of the wrapping, then she threw the paper to the ground and hugged the doll to her chest.

'Dolly,' she said over and over, her little face alight with happiness.

'Thank you, Sloan,' Teri offered. 'Jill, you haven't thanked Mr Garfield.'

'Her happiness is thanks enough.' Sloan was smiling, but there was something strange in his tone. 'There's no guile in the child.'

Yet. . . . The word was implied, but it was unspoken and Teri could hardly rise to the challenge.

You've been hurt by women, she thought. Disillusioned. She met his eyes, steady as steel, blue as the sky, disturbingly perceptive in the hard lean face. She did not try to outstare him, but turned to Jill instead and said, 'You'll have to give your doll a name, darling.'

'Miffy.' It came out unhesitatingly.

'A wonderful name!' Sloan laughed, and Teri was startled. She had heard him laugh before, but never in such genuine amusement. It was a vital sound, and extremely attractive. She was a little dazed as he went on, 'Your mommy will have tea, and I'll have a beer, and what will you have, Jill?' And as the child looked up in response to her name, 'Ice-cream?'

'Icy.' Jill's green eyes, in a smaller version of Teri's face, sparkled. 'Icy.'

'What kind?'

This time she looked at him uncomprehendingly.

'There's sherbet, peppermint, raspberry. Perhaps a float?'

All words which Jill did not know. Teri was about to say as much, when Sloan seemed to realise the fact for himself.

'How about that?' Shamelessly he gestured to a

table not far away where two teenagers sat with ice-creams before them.

Ice-cream? Glorious concoctions—sundaes, whirls of white, drenched in chocolate sauce and sprinkled with nuts. As Jill gaped, Teri felt her own mouth begin to water. She loved ice-cream with a passion, but in the last year there had been no spare penny for extravagances.

'Icy,' said Jill, pointing.

'Done.' Sloan turned to Teri. 'Have something to eat with your tea.'

'Just the tea, thank you,' she declined primly over the saliva in her mouth.

A waitress came to take the order. The pen was poised over her pad when desire gained ascendancy over dignity, and Teri said quickly, 'I've changed my mind. May I have a sundae too, please?'

They talked while they waited for the order to arrive, and discovered that they both liked swimming and cycling, music and reading; that Teri enjoyed history while Sloan preferred biography. He was not at all what she might have imagined a farmer to be. Wryly Teri acknowledged to herself that conventional stereotypes seldom approximated real life people.

There was something else she acknowledged. Sloan was an extraordinarily attractive man. She had noticed his good looks from the start, but there was more to him than a handsome face and a virile body. There was the low vital voice, the eyes that were alert and perceptive and that lit with warmth when he laughed. There was charm and humour and intelligence. And above all else, pervading all else, there was a maleness and a sexuality which seemed quite unstudied—and the more powerful for it. This man could be passionate, she knew that with sure instinct.

As before, Teri was all at once aware of a passion

within herself. It was a quality which till quite
recently she had never dreamed she possessed. It had
lain dormant, unsuspected, waiting to be roused? By
whom?

Not by Sloan! That she did know. It would be
impossible for more than one reason. Restlessly she
shifted in her seat, trying to quell a longing that
stirred within her in the strangest way.

Sloan was not for her. It had been a kind gesture on
his part to invite her to the restaurant, but it was just a
gesture nevertheless. A little treat, actual dates being
reserved for the Mirandas of his world. A little treat
for Mrs Roland's companion and her daughter—as he
saw them. She would have to tell him the truth about
Jill, the game had gone far enough.

Again she moved in her seat. Sloan was talking
about the book he was reading, a history of Linnaeus,
the famous eighteenth-century botanist who had left
his mark on the flora of the Cape. Ordinarily the
librarian in Teri would have been absorbed, for she
loved conversation about books. She heard what he
said, made the correct responses, but her mind was not
on the long-dead Linnaeus. Rather it was on the flesh-
and-blood man who sat so close to her that if she
reached out her hand she would touch his.

It occurred to her that if she had crossed the rain-
swept Johannesburg road minutes later, their first ill-
fated meeting would not have taken place. She would
have met Sloan the first time yesterday at Vins Doux,
and the hostility would have been absent from their
relationship. The challenge too. And she wondered if
she would have preferred it that way.

What a strange thought. One that she did not
continue, for at that moment the waitress came with
the tray.

The sundaes were as delicious to the tongue as they

had looked to the eye. Jill gazed at hers rapturously for a long moment before plunging in her spoon, and a sigh of delight told its own story.

For Teri the confection was an equal delight. On the day she received her first cheque she would bring Jill into town, she resolved, and sundaes would be the first of many treats. She ate slowly, relishing each spoonful, letting the ice-cream dissolve in her mouth before she swallowed. Sloan was silent now, and Teri made no attempt at conversation.

Suddenly aware that she was being watched, she looked up. Sloan's blue eyes were amused. Why, he looked as if he was actually supressing a laugh!

'What's the joke?' Teri asked.

'You don't know?' She could hear the laughter in his voice now.

He was laughing at *her*. But she did not know why.

'I seem to amuse you,' she offered uncertainly. And then, as understanding of a sort came to her, 'The sundae. . . .'

The twinkle in his eyes intensified, the lips remained still.

'Miranda wouldn't have ordered it?'

An eyebrow rose at her use of the name. 'Nor would the other women I know.'

'They'd have stuck with tea,' she acknowledged ruefully, ignoring the ridiculous pang the words "other women" evoked. 'They think of their figures.'

'Right.'

'I suppose you think I should too.'

'You wouldn't get fat if you ate a hundred sundaes—not with your build.'

And yet he was amused. Why?

'If you didn't want me to order this, you could have said so,' she said with sudden defiance. 'Anyway, I'm glad I did. I wouldn't have missed it for anything.'

'That's just it. You're enjoying it so much.' She heard a fresh bubble of laughter. 'You must know the picture you present today, Teri. A *Vogue* model, no less, soignée and elegant with that hair-style, that outfit. A lady of the world.'

'Enjoying her ice-cream like a child.' Now she did understand, and her voice was flat. 'I should have stayed with the tea after all.'

'And now you really are talking nonsense,' he said, as his hands reached across the small space between them and lifted to her head.

The action caught her so unprepared that his fingers were in her hair before her own hands could move to stop them. He was at the pins that secured the chignon. She could not get to the pins herself, instead her fingers tangled with his. Long fingers, hard yet supple, and so sensuous that she shivered as they moved against hers.

Her breath seemed to stop in her throat. Something like panic gripped her, and for a long moment her hand was quite still against his, and her body was flooded with sensation. The strangest sensation— utterly disturbing! No kiss of Andy's had ever had such an effect.

Later she would wonder how long they had actually sat like this, Sloan's hands under hers, a strange and silent conflict, while Jill continued to eat her ice-cream, oblivious of the electricity that sparked from one adult to the other. Perhaps the whole incident lasted no more than a few seconds—though it seemed like an hour—but Teri knew it would take a long time to forget it.

Abruptly she dropped her hands, and felt as if she had pulled them away from flames. Sloan's hands left her moments later, and her hair fell to her shoulders.

'Enjoy your ice-cream.' His voice was soft.

'While you laugh.' She was glad of the hair that hung like a veil about her bent head, hiding the confusion in her eyes and the warmth in her cheeks.

'While I enjoy watching a girl who looks as if she loves ice-cream.' He was not laughing now. His tone was gentle, and the more disturbing for it.

Teri went on eating the sundae, but the fun had gone out of it. The taste on her tongue was no longer her primary sensation. Rather there was an acute awareness of Sloan, and a quivering inside her body that took all her strength to conceal.

Teri finished the sundae at last, and after what seemed like eternity Jill came to the end of hers. They were free to leave the restaurant, to emerge into the sunlight and the bustle of a busy Cape Town street.

Teri stole a glance at Sloan as they walked to the car. Only his profile was visible some way above her. He looked cool and calm. Nothing in his demeanour suggested that in the last half hour something had happened to disturb him. In the restaurant the air between them had seemed to vibrate with electricity, she had felt as if her hand could touch it. She had thought that he must feel it too. It came to her now that Sloan had felt nothing at all.

He did not speak on the way back to Vins Doux. He looked preoccupied, Teri thought, and she was glad of it, because it meant she did not need to make small-talk. While they had waited for their order to arrive, conversation had been easy, fluent and flowing, arising out of common interests and an enjoyable stimulation.

And then he had loosened her hair, and she had trembled at the touch of his fingers, and suddenly everything had changed. Part of her wanted to think about what had happened, another part rejected the very idea. Sloan was not her type, his unexpected gentleness in the restaurant notwithstanding, and the less she thought about him the better. If only she could stop herself thinking about him altogether!

Jill sat on the back seat, playing with Miffi, murmuring to her, telling her it was time to sleep. At length the murmurings grew fainter, then stopped. Glancing backward over her shoulder, Teri saw that her sister had fallen asleep. The unaccustomed excitement of the day coupled with the purring movement of the car had been too much for her.

With the doll hugged against her chest, and smears of ice-cream around her mouth, Jill was the picture of a contented child. Teri couldn't help smiling. In just one day the little girl had had more pleasure at Vins Doux than she had experienced in all the months since her parents had died. And there would be other good times for her, Teri knew. As far as Jill was concerned the decision to come to the Cape had been the right one.

She turned back, her eyes alighting on the rugged face of the driver as she did so. The smile faded from her lips as a question came into her mind. 'Was the decision the right one for me?'

The aroma of newly-ground coffee was in the air as Teri and Jill walked through the doors of the sun-room next morning. Supper was eaten in the dining-room, but Emma liked to have breakfast in the glassed-in room on the east side, where the sun streamed through the windows for most of the day. The room had been added on to the house in recent years. Plants were everywhere, philodendrons trailed over white trellises, a group of cacti stood prickly stiff on a windowsill, and in a corner an azalea was just coming into delicate pink flower. Unlike the rest of the house, where the furniture was mostly antique, here the tables and chairs were of cane, and a red and white cloth patterned in a bold African design covered the table. Teri knew that after the library this room would be her favourite.

She was smiling as she came into the room where Emma was pouring coffee. 'Good morning, I'm so sorry I'm late. This air is just. . . .' She stopped. Sloan was at the table, she wondered why she had not seen him immediately.

'You're not late at all, dears.' Emma's smile was warm and forgiving. 'Come and sit down and help yourselves to some scones. They're still warm from the oven.'

'The air is just what?' Sloan asked.

'Intoxicating,' Teri answered after a moment. 'I've heard of air like champagne and never known what it meant, and now I do know, because I think I feel a little drunk on it. I haven't slept this late in ages!'

She wondered if the words hid her feeling of awkwardness. On waking she had taken a shower before dressing in jeans and a plaid shirt. Her hair hung loose around her shoulders, and her only concession to make-up was a touch of gloss at her lips. A glance in the mirror had shown her a girl who looked much younger than her years, a very different image from the one she had presented to Sloan a day earlier. Her appearance should not matter, yet for some reason it did. Even in casual trousers and open-necked shirt Sloan looked so ruggedly in control of himself that she thought regretfully of yesterday's image. It had been a mask of a kind, a façade from behind which she could try to meet him on equal terms.

Which was nonsense. She was what she was, and neither clothes nor make-up could, nor should, make a difference. So deciding, she took a scone from the basket, buttered it with careful fingers, and put it on Jill's new red plastic plate.

'I hope you'll sleep late often, Teri,' said Emma. 'By the way, Sloan, did I tell you that I'd heard from Bruce and Virginia? They'll be arriving some time this afternoon.'

'Ah.'

In the act of buttering a scone for herself, Teri looked up, caught by an inflection in Sloan's tone. His face was devoid of expression. He was leaning back in his chair, hands spread casually before him, his pose relaxed. And yet Teri would have said he was anything but relaxed, and she wondered how she knew it.

'My niece and nephew,' Emma explained, turning to her.

'They're coming to stay at Vins Doux?' Teri was curious at this first mention of Emma's family.

'Yes.' Emma took the coffee-pot and topped up a cup that was almost full. 'Sloan, you *will* join us for dinner?'

'I'll be here.'

Not for the first time Teri was struck by what seemed the curious relationship between the two. Emma seemed almost to defer to Sloan. Her manner with other members of her staff, though always friendly, was different.

'I thought we'd eat around seven-thirty. That will give us time. . . .' She stopped.

Time for what? Teri wondered idly, only to sit up in her chair as Emma went on, 'You'll take Teri with you this morning, Sloan?'

'I don't need to do any more shopping.' The words came out too quickly.

'Sloan is going to show you around Vins Doux,' Emma said.

Somehow Teri managed to bite back the word 'no' that came so instinctively to her lips. Instead she said quietly, 'I've already seen the house and the vineyards.'

'You didn't get very far,' Sloan observed.

His mouth had taken on the amused slant that she was beginning to know, and the eyes that held hers were faintly sardonic. He knows, Teri thought, he knows how I feel about going with him.

'I don't think Jill could manage it,' she said, refusing to give him the satisfaction of being the first to look away.

'Jill can spend the morning with me,' said Emma. 'And if I get tired, Jessie will look after her.

Sloan grinned. 'I thought we'd go on horseback.'

She could say that she didn't ride, and he would tell her that he would teach her. Besides, Emma was aware of the new breeches reposing in Teri's wardrobe, for she had urged her to include them in her purchases. Teri looked from one to the other and knew it would be better to save her excuses for an occasion when she had more chance of getting her way. And she tried to quell the quiver of excitement, the quite unjustified quiver of excitement, that flicked through her at the idea of being alone with Sloan. It was even possible that she would enjoy herself.

She *was* enjoying herself, she decided half an hour later. It was her first time on a horse, but far from being nervous, as Emma had thought she might be, Teri felt exhilarated. To riding born, she thought joyfully, and knew she would do this again, and often.

She had caught back her hair in a scarlet snood that matched the red in the plaid of her shirt, and she laughed as she felt the wind seize it and play with it. Beneath her the motion of the mare Sloan had chosen for her was gentle and rhythmic, and ahead of her was Sloan himself, tall and supple on his own horse. He turned around as the wind threw the sound of her laughter towards him. On his face was a question, but she smiled and shook her head.

She had been a fool even to think twice about letting him show her around. The air was crisp and sweet, and on either side of the trail the vineyards stretched all the way to the mountains. They had ridden some way through an estate that was even bigger than she had imagined. New vistas enfolded constantly, enchanting Teri at every bend of the trail.

And all the while she was aware of the man on the horse just yards in front of her. Even when her eyes were on the vineyards, on the bunches of grapes that would ripen and be made into wine, she was aware of Sloan. With a slight sense of shock she realised that she did not need to see his face to know how he looked. The supple build, the rugged features, all were imprinted on her mind as clearly as words are in print on the pages of a book.

How had such a thing happened? And so quickly? It must be the air. She had told Emma and Sloan that it made her feel drunk, perhaps it also made her perceptions more acute. Andy's features would be just as clear to her.   Closing her eyes, Teri focused on Andy. There was an impression of kindness, of sheer niceness. Of a round face and sandy hair. And that was all. A little shocked, Teri looked again at the figure in front of her, and then, with an effort this time, she forced her attention back to the vineyards.

At the wine cellars they reined in the horses. Sloan dismounted quickly, and as she saw him come to her Teri made to do the same. But he was quicker than she was, and his hands were on her waist, lifting her down.

She thought he would release her as her feet touched the ground, but he did not do so immediately. He stood close to her, very close, his hands on her waist, his fingers spreading down towards her hips. She looked up at him, and found that he was looking at her. He was very tall, taller than she had realised, and though only his hands were touching her, in some strange way she seemed to have contact with every inch of his body. Yesterday, in the restaurant, she had experienced a strange longing. Now as she saw his eyes on her lips, she felt it again, the same feeling but stronger, and her heart was pounding hard against her ribs.

She dropped her eyes to his mouth. How would it feel on hers? She was insane even to wonder! One man's lips were surely much like another's, she had been kissed by Andy and by other men before him. How could she be so certain that Sloan's kiss would be different?

The hands on her waist tightened a fraction, the movement bringing her closer to him. She could feel every one of his fingers, they seemed to burn through her shirt on to her skin. After a moment he let her go—and she didn't know if she was relieved or disappointed. 'What a mixed-up creature I am!' she thought in disgust.

In the cellars it was dark. There was a pungent smell that Teri would forever associate with the making of wine. And with Sloan.

She thought she would not be able to concentrate as Sloan explained to her the various processes through which the grapes must go before wine is bottled. Yet in no time her interest was caught, and as they went from one part of the cellars to the next, she followed him, listening to his explanations with rapt attention.

He spoke easily, he had the ability to make what he said absorbing. Teri hung on his words with as much fascination as when they had discussed mutual interests in the restaurant.

SERPENT IN PARADISE 71

'You make a good tour guide,' she observed at length, as she watched bottles emerge corked and labelled.

'Thank you, kind lady. All the more reason for me to let you complete the tour in time-honoured fashion.' Teri gave a puzzled look and Sloan laughed. 'Wine-tasting is what we generally keep for last.'

Generally.... How many others had gone with Sloan on this tour? And how many of them had been women? Firmly she pushed the question from her mind.

'Last and best, I hope,' she responded with a little laugh of her own.

'That's for you to decide. Well, what will it be? White wine or red? Where does your fancy lie, Teri?'

She loved wine, but she was no connoisseur. She looked at the bottles, the white wines, the Rieslings, a clear amber colour. The roses, darker than blood, sparkling. He was waiting for her to choose.

'Red,' she suggested.

Sloan decanted the wine into a small crystal wine-glass. She watched him take a sip. 'Another of our customs,' he grinned. 'Your turn now, Teri.'

She waited for him to fill up a second glass, but he did not. Instead he reached the glass to her, holding on to it when she would have taken it from him. He lifted it to her lips, and now he was again very close to her.

She felt his hand touch her chin. The touch was like a caress—a caress, the dominant quality of which was not warmth but sensuousness. Involuntarily Teri's eyes went up, and as her eyes met Sloan's the breath skittered in her throat. She took a sip of the wine and did not taste it. It was as if the only taste her senses could perceive was that which his lips had left on the glass.

'Like it?' he asked softly.

'Yes,' she said unsteadily, and knew that if they were talking of the wine they were also talking of something else. 'Do you?'

He did not answer for a moment. A long moment in which he studied her face as intently as if he were committing every feature to memory, before he dropped his eyes to her throat where a pulse beat madly, and to the outline of her breasts straining beneath a shirt that was a little damp from the exertion of the ride. Then he said, 'Why not?' And, giving her no time to ponder the strange turn of phrase, 'Want some more?'

Teri had never felt more uncertain of herself. 'I'm not sure.'

'You don't know what you want, Teri? I'd have thought you did—most of the time.' His voice was rough, and now he had lost her. She knew he was alluding to something, and wished she knew what.

She didn't know what made her say, 'Do you always know what *you* want?'

'Yes. And when I want something I make a habit of getting it.' There was something dangerous in his tone.

'At any cost?' She was breathless.

'Sometimes. But I do have rules, and I play by them. I wonder if you play by the same rules, Teri?'

CHAPTER FIVE

SHE felt suddenly frightened. There was a harshness in Sloan's tone which she could not explain, a meaning to his words which she did not understand. Whatever it was he was trying to say, it was not clear to her. She was about to ask him what he was getting at when he asked, 'Well, will you have more wine?'

'No, thanks.'

'You said you liked it.'

Perhaps he did not understand her in turn, did not know that her refusal stemmed from the fact that his manner called for defiance.

'Not that much.'

He shrugged and put the glass back on the table. 'Round one, two and three to you,' Teri thought as they walked to the door, 'but this round was mine, even if I won it only at the end.'

The end of what. A battle? Yesterday she had taken his change of mood for a truce. He had been so nice. No, not nice, for that was a word which could never be applied to Sloan. He had been generous to Jill, amusing with Teri herself. Today he had been informative—and seductive. Seductive above all else.

She had not imagined the message in the spreading fingers, in the eyes that had lingered on her face and body. She had been excited by the message. There had even been a moment, earlier, when if Sloan had tried to kiss her he would have met with no resistance.

And now it seemed there was a battle after all. Why? she wondered, as they emerged from the cellars and she blinked her eyes against the sudden dazzle of the

sun. She could think of nothing she had done to
offend Sloan. Except to throw mud at his car. Could
he still be nursing a grudge over the incident? Surely
not! Sloan was not a man who would sulk or hold on
to a grudge. And then again, perhaps he was. It was
possible that she had been taken in by the vital
appearance, and had misjudged him.

They came to the horses, and this time Teri
mounted quickly, escaping the hands that might
otherwise have helped her. She told herself that she
did not want to experience their touch again so soon.
Preferably never, she amended firmly.

With the tour of the cellars at an end, she imagined
they would ride back the way they had come, but
Sloan set his horse in a new direction, and with no
orders from Teri the mare followed suit.

The trail went some way through the vineyards
before the scenery changed. They were in open veld
now, a windswept area on the slope of a hill. A few
stunted trees dotted the slope. Here and there aloes
grew, the waxy-tinged flowers a dusty mauve.

Glancing at the tall figure in front of her, Teri
wondered at his thoughts. Since leaving the cellars
Sloan had not turned in his seat, had not uttered a
word. Why did his moods keep changing? Would she
ever grow to understand him? Did she want to?

Restlessly she shifted position. There were things
Sloan did not know about her. He thought that Jill
was her child, no doubt he had endowed Teri with an
illicit and exciting past. It was time to tell him the
truth. Perhaps if he saw that she was honest with him,
his own attitude towards her would change.

They rode farther, and the terrain became more
inhospitable. Were they still on Vins Doux land? Even
if they were, the tour had obviously ended. Teri
wondered why they were going this way.

At the brow of the hill Sloan halted his horse and turned. Seeing him dismount, Teri did likewise, quickly again, and knew from the twist of his mouth that he understood the reason for her haste.

A little uneasy all at once, she asked, 'Why did you bring me here?'

He shrugged and gestured. 'There's a good view of the valley. Not far to walk.'

The view was indeed good, Teri acknowledged minutes later, as she surveyed a vista of vineyards, stretching as far as the eye could see. Yet she could not shake off the feeling that Sloan had had a motive in bringing her here. There had been other views, not unlike this one. . . .

She turned her head, suddenly, hoping to catch him unawares. She did not have far to look, because he was close beside her—a little too close for her comfort— and she could see that his eyes were hard.

'Why *did* you bring me here?' she asked again.

'To talk.'

'About books and music?' she asked lightly, concealing her growing apprehension.

'Hardly.' The word confirmed what she already knew. Sloan had the look of a man with things on his mind, and a cosy chat was not one of them.

'I don't think we've anything else to talk about.'

'And there you're wrong, Teri.' His voice was soft, dangerous.

Finding herself unequal to holding the gaze of eyes that were now like steel, she looked away. Not far away an eagle soared in the sky, and she envied the bird its freedom. If only she could get away from this spot with the same ease, away from this man!

It was very quiet on the hill, so quiet that one could hear the wild grasses moving if one listened. What did Sloan want to discuss?

'The mud I threw at your car. You still haven't forgiven me for that?'

He gave a short laugh. 'Not on the agenda for today. Though we'll still deal with it.' He paused. When he went on his voice had changed. It had become deadly serious. 'Tell me about your friendship with Emma.'

This was why he had brought her here? Amazed, she spun round.

'You know about it already.'

'Tell me again anyway,' he invited.

'We met in a supermarket. Emma had fallen and I happened to be there. We became friends. When she decided to return to the Cape she asked me to come with her. That's all there is.'

'No,' he said, and now his voice was even more dangerous, 'I think there's more.'

'Perhaps *you* should tell *me*,' Teri said after a moment.

'Perhaps I should. There's a girl in this story, Teri, a girl who's been buying a great many clothes lately, and only the most expensive.'

Anger stirred in Teri. How dared Sloan appoint himself as judge over what she wore and what she spent!

'You haven't seen half of them,' she threw at him tautly.

'I've no doubt that's true. Whose money went into the purchase of those clothes, Teri?'

'You're suggesting it wasn't my own.'

'I know it wasn't.'

'I earned a living before I came here,' she pointed out very quietly, over the anger that was beginning to assume the proportions of a veld-fire.

'So you did, and you budgeted carefully. The girl who threw mud at my car was furious because her pretty dress was the only good one she possessed.'

The gist of the conversation was becoming clearer by the minute. 'I could have lied to you about that. You were furious too, and I had to find a reason to excuse my behaviour.'

'You're still budgeting,' he pointed out. 'You couldn't afford to buy your daughter a small doll. You stint yourself on ice-cream when it's obvious you love it. I think you live from one pay-cheque to the next.'

'What if I do?' Her voice rose in the anger she could no longer suppress. 'There are millions of women out there who struggle to manage on what they earn. Do you think there's some shame in that, Mr Garfield?'

'On the contrary, I respect people who work hard for what they have. Who have to balance their priorities.' His tone changed. 'I'd be a fool if I didn't.'

I'm the fool, she thought bitterly. I fell for what I thought was your generosity—and all the while the whole thing was a trap.

'You trapped me yesterday,' she said aloud.

'It didn't start out that way. I don't expect you to believe me.'

I believed you yesterday. I believed that you bought the doll for Jill just because you wanted to see a small girl happy. I believed that you treated us to the ice-creams for the same reason. Worst of all, when you let down my hair and spoke to me in a special kind of tone, I believed that you found me attractive, desirable. God help me, I believed I'd misjudged you before, I believed that there could be something between you and me, something good. . . . I must have been insane!

'I don't believe you,' she said coolly over the pain in her throat.

'Emma did buy clothes for you and Jill?'

'She gave me the money for them, yes.' Teri met Sloan's eyes squarely. 'She wanted us to look nice at

Vins Doux, to be dressed appropriately. Is that so difficult to understand?'

'And you went the whole hog and bought the most expensive things you could find.'

All along she had got the impression that he was looking at her clothes. Now she knew why.

'She wanted us to look nice,' she said again.

'You make it sound so simple.'

'It *is* simple.'

'The way you put it—yes.'

The blue eyes had lost none of their hardness, the long line of jaw was relentlessly set. Contempt seemed to be etched in every line of the hard-boned tanned face. He was not convinced.

'Do you think,' Teri asked slowly, disbelievingly, 'that I conned Emma into giving me things?'

'It has crossed my mind.' Flatly. With no hint of apology.

This can't be happening to me, Teri thought wildly. Coming to Vins Doux was such a wonderful opportunity, and now it was turning into a nightmare. She looked at Sloan, and to her horror tears filled her eyes before she could do anything to prevent them. She felt her lips quiver.

My God, he mustn't see me like this, she thought. He mustn't know what he's doing to me.

Abruptly she bent her head, wishing that her hair hung loose today, for it would conceal her distress.

She jerked when a hand went beneath her chin. She tried to pull away, but the grip was strong. No seductive tenderness in the fingers this time. Sloan was forcing her to look at him.

His eyes held a strange expression. The contempt was still there, but there was something else as well, as if Sloan Garfield had caught a glimpse of something he had not expected to see. Teri was too overwrought to put a name to the expression. She did not even try.

'Let go of me!'

'The innocent,' he drawled.

'What!'

'The picture of distraught young innocence.' His voice became harsh. 'Innocence is the one thing you don't possess, Teri.'

Just for a moment she was bewildered. And then she realised that he was talking about Jill. All morning she had intended telling him the truth about her sister, but the moment for that had passed. Sloan did not deserve her honesty.

She forced herself to smile. It was a smile that was totally foreign to her, feminine and provocative and all-knowing. She had no idea that with the tears clinging to her lashes its effect was devastating.

'You're right, Sloan, I'm not innocent.'

His voice was harsher than she had heard it. 'Emma must have been a pushover! For a moment you nearly had *me* fooled.'

'What a moment that would have been!' She was on dangerous ground now, but anger was spurring her on. 'You're not used to being fooled, are you, Sloan?'

She was bracing herself for another verbal rebuff, bracing herself to meet it, when merciless hands pulled her up against him. She tried to twist away, and knew the struggle was unequal as she did so. His hands cupped her head, clamping it between his strong palms. He looked down at her a moment, his eyes as searching as if they could see to the depths of her soul. She heard him laugh harshly, and then his mouth had found hers and was savaging it with ruthless intensity. For a moment Teri couldn't think, couldn't breathe. There was only awareness of the cruel mouth on hers, of the hard legs and thighs pushed against her own soft ones. With a rush her senses sprang into vivid life. As his lips forcibly parted hers, she felt dizzy.

And then, quite suddenly, outrage took over. Later she would wonder why it had taken so long to surface. As Sloan lifted his mouth to breathe it was that outrage which gave her the strength to push herself out of his grip.

'Was that a demonstration of your brute power?' she demanded over the thunder in her ears.

Beneath his tan he was a little pale, otherwise he was perfectly composed. 'It's my way of telling you that I'm not a man to be fooled with.'

Which she knew already. Just as she knew that she had never been quite so excited.

'And that I won't allow defenceless people to be fooled either,' he added.

'As I have an eye to the main chance you'll have to watch me carefully, won't you?' she taunted, throwing the words at him as she made for her horse.

'Wait!' he commanded.

'Not for you!' she shouted without slowing her step. Lightning-swift, she mounted the mare and spurred her back along the trail. Though she knew that Sloan would catch up with her in minutes she did not stop to look back.

There was a car in the drive, one she did not recognise. Walking rapidly back to the house from the stables, Teri stopped short. Was Emma Roland entertaining guests?

Then she remembered Bruce and Virginia, the nephew and niece who were due to arrive today. She had thought they were coming in the late afternoon; obviously they had arrived already.

Pushing her hands through hair that had loosened

from the snood, Teri knew she looked a mess. Not that it mattered that her hair had been tangled by the wind, or that her shirt had worked loose from her jeans, those were imperfections easily excused and explained. Harder to explain were the ravages to her face. A tentative lick at her lips told her they were swollen from Sloan's kisses, and the tears that she had failed to check on the crazy ride back to the house would have made telltale tracks on dusty cheeks.

She could not put on a pretence of polite sociability for Bruce and Virginia. More important, she could not face Emma. If the elderly woman was tactful enough to withhold comment, one look at Terri's face would lead her to draw conclusions, and essentially they would be the right ones.

Emma would be upset when she learned of Sloan's behaviour. Nothing could excuse his words or actions. As Emma's employee he would surely be told to pack his bags. Teri tried to suppress the knowledge that Emma held Sloan in great esteem, and that she would be sorry to see the back of him.

Teri told herself that she did not care what happened to Sloan. He had behaved outrageously, and if he was fired that was no more than he deserved. But she was not quite ready to tell Emma what had happened. First she had to come to terms with certain aspects of the incident in her own mind.

Hoping she had not already been seen, she changed course and entered the house through a side door. She breathed a little sigh of relief when she reached her room without seeing a soul. For once the sight of the room, with its lovely colour-scheme and beautiful furniture, gave her no joy. Breathing hard, she sank down on her bed—and then jumped to her feet as she remembered Jill. With a little stab of remorse she realised that she had not given the child a thought all morning.

'Have you made me forget the things that matter, Sloan Garfield?' she asked aloud into the silent room.

Jill was in the garden. Teri could see her from the window which overlooked a wide stretch of green lawn. Jessie, a quiet sweet-faced maid, was with her, as was a puppy, a gambolling ball of fluff which would soon grow into a pedigree collie. Miffi, the rubber doll—Teri felt a pang of bitterness at sight of her—lay forgotten on the grass, while the puppy and the little girl ran circles around each other. Even from a distance the air rang with the sound of the dog's excited yelping and the laughter of the child. It would be difficult to say which of the two was enjoying the game more.

It was a game of tag of which neither seemed to tire, and which could have no victory, for the two seemed evenly matched. And then, rather incredibly, Jill managed to catch hold of the puppy's tail, and the resulting excitement increased in pitch. Through the rawness of her own emotions Teri smiled.

Leaving the window, she sat down at the dressing-table. The face that stared back at her was that of a stranger. More than the dishevelled hair and swollen lips which she had expected, it was the eyes which she did not recognise. There was a wildness in them, and also a hunger. There was turbulence in those eyes, and emotions which looked like erupting.

This can't be me! Teri thought, appalled, staring at the furious sensuous being in the mirror. I've never looked like this in my life. And she knew that there had never before been a Sloan Garfield in her life. There had never been a man who could make her feel quite so vitally alive as she had been in those moments when he had kissed her.

There had never been a man whom she so hated.

Picking up her brush, she began to restore her hair

to its usual smoothness with long fierce strokes. The repetition of the movement had a calming effect, and slowly the wildness began to fade from her eyes, if not from her soul.

On her way to the room she had thought she would leave Vins Doux, but on reflection she knew she would not do so. She had made a commitment to Emma Roland, and it would not be fair to her friend to leave her now. Nor would it be fair to Jill to take her from this place where in so short a time she was already beginning to show signs of getting better.

But is it fair that I should have to stay? a small voice asked. Fair that at best my peace of mind will be shattered, at worst my world might never be quite the same again?

The brush-strokes became fiercer still as Teri pushed the stirrings of self-pity from her mind. She had never been a quitter, why start now? Besides, if she were to leave Vins Doux, Sloan would know why, and the knowledge would give him satisfaction. That would not do. She would have to make the best of things—given the beauty of Vins Doux, surely only a determined martyr would find that a difficult feat.

Fighting spirit to the fore now, she showered, and exchanged jeans and shirt for a pale blue sun-dress. Then she left the house and gathered a protesting Jill for her midday nap.

The little girl settled, Teri went in search of Emma and found her in the sun-room where lunch had been served the previous day.

'Enjoy your tour with Sloan?' Emma looked up from the wall-hanging, two rows of which had already been hooked.

After just a moment's hesitation, Teri said carefully, 'It was very interesting.'

The older woman's eyes skimmed her face a

moment, then returned to her work as she said, 'I'm glad. As time passes I hope you'll learn a lot more about wine-making.'

What would you say, Teri wondered, if you knew how close I was half an hour ago to leaving Vins Doux?

Aloud she said, 'I hope so too. I was wondering what you'd like me to do.'

Emma lifted her eyes once more, and this time they were twinkling. 'For a start, why don't you sit down? Virginia and Bruce have arrived—did you know?—and when they come from their rooms we'll have lunch.'

Sloan. Would he also be here to welcome the new arrivals? Teri felt a quick twinge of panic. It was one thing to have decided to see things out at Vins Doux, quite another to face Sloan again so soon.

'I'm not very hungry,' she said uncertainly. 'Would you mind very much if I skipped lunch today?'

The grey eyes went to her face once more, thoughtfully, lingering longer this time. She knows, Teri thought, she knows what happened today.

That being the case, this was the perfect moment to complain about Sloan. Teri opened her mouth, only to close it again. She would say what she had to, but not now. She could not have explained, even to herself, why the time was not right.

'Of course you don't have to have lunch if you don't want to,' Emma said very gently. 'You can meet Virginia and Bruce later, at dinner.'

'Thank you, I'd prefer that.'

'We'll be dressing up tonight, Teri.'

'A party?'

This time it was Emma's turn to hesitate before answering. 'It's a rather special occasion.'

Teri knew her friend well enough by now not to ask

further questions. She would know the reason in good
time.

'Why don't you spend the afternoon exploring?'
Emma suggested. 'You seem to enjoy being out of
doors.'

'Don't you have something for me to do?'

'No, dear, I don't. I told you before that I'm not an
invalid needing constant attention.'

'I know that.' Green eyes were troubled. 'I'd love to
explore, it's the most beautiful place I've ever seen,
but I feel I'm doing nothing to earn my salary.'

Emma smiled. 'I'll tell you when I need you. Jessie
seems to have appointed herself Jill's nanny and she's
a good soul, so the little one is in good hands. If you
want to venture farther afield you're free to take the
red Mini, I'll give you a spare set of keys.' More
softly, she said, 'Enjoy yourself, Teri. You deserve it.'

Teri parked the Mini at the top of the cliff and took
the path that led down to the beach. Kicking off her
sandals, she let her feet sink down into sand that was
soft and deliciously sun-warmed. Before her was the
ocean. The tide was in, the waves rising high before
crashing on to rocks and shore in foaming thunder.

Teri had taken up Emma's suggestion to explore
because she wanted to be alone. The encounter with
Sloan had raised unsettling emotions, and she needed
to come to terms with them.

The beach was almost deserted. The dearth of
footmarks attested to the fact that few people came
this way, but in the distance, on a jagged outcropping
of rock, a lone fisherman cast his line. Gulls swooped
about him, and Teri, girl of the interior and for too
long starved of the sight of the ocean, thought what a
lovely picture they made. On another day she would
have searched in her bag for paper and pencil, would

have tried her hand at a sketch. But not today.

Today was for thinking. She lay down near the water and closed her eyes, letting the sun warm her face and the sand sift through her fingers.

She could have dealt with anger if that was the only emotion Sloan aroused in her, but there were other emotions which gave her more concern. An excitement when he kissed her. A surging primitive awareness of being female. A strange longing which had survived despite her outrage at the arrogance of his behaviour. It was a longing which was still with her now, however much she tried to deny the fact to herself.

She had come to the beach to sort out her emotions—and it came to her gradually that she could not do so. How could she, when she did not even understand them?

The simplest way of dealing with the matter would be to leave Vins Doux, but that was an idea which she had already rejected. She had made up her mind to stay. That being the case she must decide how to deal with Sloan.

And how to deal with myself, said an insistent voice. I can't let myself go to pieces every time I see him. That path can only lead to destruction. Nor can I avoid him, as I'd first thought possible. Sloan has a special place at Vins Doux. I must find a way of living with the situation. I *will* find it. Somehow.

And Sloan must never know the effect he has on me. If he did, his power would be absolute.

Opening her eyes, she came abruptly to her feet. The wind was in her hair as she began to walk, keeping close to the water-line. The incoming waves hit the shore and became foam, curling around her ankles, and the taste of salt was strong on her lips. The fisherman seemed to have made a catch, for he was unhooking something from his rod, and Teri wondered whether his wife would be glad, or whether she would mind having to clean the fish.

What a lovely spot this was! She walked as fast as was possible on the golden beach sand, and gradually she felt the tension drain away from her. She would come here with Emma and Jill, and she and Emma would sit and chat or read while Jill made sand-castles.

Jill would thrive here, she could hardly do otherwise. Teri had been foolish even to consider letting Sloan deprive her sister of these surroundings.

Her equilibrium regained, she made her way back to Vins Doux at last. Save for the clatter of dishes in the region of the kitchen, the house seemed deserted. Teri glanced at her watch, and wondered if Emma and her relatives had begun to dress for supper. She had stayed away longer than she had intended, and she quickened her step as she made her way to her room.

Jill was already dressed. Jessie had chosen a pink dress with a wide gathered skirt and smocked top, and now she was brushing the little girl's hair.

'Jill looks lovely,' Teri said gratefully. 'Thanks so much for looking after her.'

Jessie tied a pink ribbon Alice-style around the small head, then left the room with the gentle smile that had endeared her to both sisters alike. It was Teri's turn to get dressed.

The choice was surprisingly difficult. Sloan's remarks earlier in the day made her want to choose the simplest of her new dresses, something demure and plain and relatively inexpensive. Anything to deflect his scorn and keep attention away from herself.

And then the fighting spirit which never deserted Teri for long came once more to the fore. Why pander to Sloan? Her eyes lit with mischief as she decided upon the rust chiffon. It was a dress she had hesitated

over in the shop, though the saleslady had raved over
it, and she had seen herself that it suited her. It was a
dress that hinted and promised without being explicit
or vulgar. It was the dress of a temptress.

The effect was heightened by hair that had been
quickly washed and dried on Teri's return from the
beach, and which now hung in a smooth curve just
touching her shoulders, and by eyes which had been
provocatively shaded and darkened. It was an effect
that was at once elegant and provocative. It would not
be lost on Sloan, Teri thought grimly.

Voices came from the dining-room, the sound of
talking, and then a burst of laughter. A low laugh
which Teri recognised, and a high brittle one which
she did not. For a moment she felt unnerved, then she
lifted her shoulders and put a smile on her face, and
walked into the room with Jill.

They were all at the far end of the room, pouring
drinks, and for a few moments Teri's entrance was
unobserved. She stood quite still, taking in the scene.
Emma, in a gown of midnight blue, stood talking to a
dark-haired young man. A few feet away was Sloan. A
girl was beside him, her auburn head thrown
vivaciously back, her hand on his arm as she laughed
up at him. He was smiling down at her, absorbed in
her, Teri thought, and his face had none of the
familiar mockery.

She caught her breath as pain knifed through her,
unexpected and swift. The moment passed, but Teri
felt weak. I can't be jealous, she thought numbly. Not
of Sloan. Oh God, please, not of Sloan!

CHAPTER SIX

EMMA looked up suddenly and saw her, and a moment later the others saw her too. Silence fell. Teri stiffened, her hand gripped Jill's more tightly, and the smile on her lips felt as if it had been pasted there.

And then Emma was moving towards her, holding out her hand, drawing her into the group. 'Teri dear, I want you to meet Virginia and Bruce Mansfield, my nephew and niece. Ginny, Bruce.... This is Teri Malloy.'

'The companion,' said Virginia. She was a striking-looking girl, but the smile that revealed perfect teeth did not reach her eyes, Teri noticed.

'And my very dear friend.' Emma's tone had the slightest edge of sharpness.

'Glad to meet you,' Bruce said, giving her a look that was decidedly male, though not blatant. 'Good choice, Aunt Emma.'

'Thank you, dear,' Teri heard her friend say lightly, and involuntarily her eyes went to Sloan.

His scrutiny *was* blatant, missing not a line of the body revealed by the seductive dress. She saw his eyes rest on the shadowed valley between her breasts, saw them slide to her hips and her thighs, and she thought suddenly how stupid she had been—she should have worn the demure dress after all. His eyes lifted, travelled up to her face, and she saw the return of the mocking glitter that she hated.

A spark of challenge surged once more through Teri's veins. She had been right to wear the dress, there was no need to play herself down! Lifting her chin, she danced Sloan her most provocative smile before saying primly, 'I'm not so sure Sloan approves.'

There! The ball was in his court. Virginia sent her a hard puzzled look as Sloan's lips tilted in a wicked grin. 'Who says I don't approve?' he drawled, his tone so suggestive that only someone very naïve would have misunderstood his meaning.

Cheeks flaming, Teri glared at him. Their battle had been brought into the open this morning. It was clear that Sloan would use every means at his disposal to humiliate her. Had they been alone she would have slapped him, very hard, and taken joy in seeing him humiliated in his turn. As it was, she was glad when Emma said gently, 'What will you have to drink, Teri? Nothing? You're sure? Then why don't we sit down and start dinner?'

The table was even more festive than usual, and the meal was delicious. Lightly poached asparagus was followed by a wonderful salmon, but Teri hardly tasted her food. She pushed it around on her plate, hoping nobody would notice, and then she looked up, found Sloan's eyes on her, and knew that he at least was aware of how little she ate. With determination she speared a piece of salmon and made herself swallow it.

Jill was on one side of her, Bruce was on the other. After a minute or two Teri realised that she was to be spared the effort of making small talk with him. He did not seem interested in her, but was absorbed instead in an anecdote Sloan was recounting.

Teri had met enough men like Bruce to recognise the type. His response to the initial introduction had been mechanically male and gallant, that was all. Bruce was a man who would be attracted to girls who were scintillating and sophisticated, a little like his sister. Teri did not mind his lack of interest—if anything she was relieved.

She was trying to adjust herself to the atmosphere, and finding it surprisingly difficult. There was conversation, light and sparkling, conducted mainly by Sloan and Virginia with Bruce interjecting pieces of quick repartee. And through it all, there was a sense of separateness, as if each person at the table was playing a part in a play.

Sloan laughed once at a joke Virginia had made, and Teri's glance went to his face. With a sense of shock she saw that his eyes were not amused at all, that there was a hardness in the line of his jaw. There was something strange about Sloan tonight, Teri could not have said what it was.

Come to think of it, Sloan was not the only strange one at the table. Though on the surface Emma was her usual friendly self, she was also withdrawn. Looking at her, Teri saw that she was preoccupied, and she wondered why. As for the guests—Bruce seemed bored, as if he had come to Vins Doux under duress, and Virginia was so vivacious and brittle that she began to get on Teri's nerves.

Virginia turned to Emma, almost as if she suddenly thought it her duty to include her aunt in the conversation. 'Is it good to be back at Vins Doux?'

'Very good.'

'Why did you stay away so long?'

'I needed a change.' Emma's tone was light.

'I've never been to Johannesburg—did the City of Gold live up to your expectations?' Bruce asked.

'In some ways.'

'What did you do there?' Virginia was curious.

'Amongst other things, I saw a way of life I'd never known. I twisted my ankle and I made two friends.'

Emma smiled at Teri, and Virginia caught the

smile and said, 'So that's where you found your companion.'

'I found a friend,' Emma corrected her gently. 'Two very dear friends.'

There was a moment of silence, then Virginia, voice higher now, said, 'Your attitudes seem to have changed, Aunt Emma. You used to have such high moral expectations of all the world.'

No mistaking her meaning! Teri's cheeks flamed and she marvelled at the girl's rudeness. If anything, Virginia did not look the sort who would wait for marriage to sleep with any man who took her fancy.

'Perhaps I'm more modern than you realise.' Emma's tone had lost none of its gentleness, but to Teri the rebuke was apparent. She shot her friend a grateful look. It was not Emma's fault that Teri had embroiled herself in a lie that now seemed foolish, but it was generous of her to play along with it all the same. She would have to tell them all the truth about Jill, but she would have to choose the right opportunity to do so.

Virginia resented her presence here—that much seemed obvious. What was less obvious was why. But there was no time to think about it, for Bruce, as if to divert attention from his sister, had changed the subject. 'What decided you to come back here?' he wanted to know.

Emma exchanged a glance with Sloan before saying, 'It was time. And Vins Doux is my home, Bruce dear, why don't you pour yourself some more wine? And Virginia's glass is empty too, I think.'

Neatly done, Teri thought, for by the time Bruce had poured the wine the conversation had changed direction and he did not return to his question. Beneath Emma's unassuming exterior there was a woman who knew how to handle herself.

There are undercurrents at this table, Teri thought again. At first I thought I was imagining it, but I wasn't. There are definite undercurrents, and Emma and Sloan are at the centre of them.

Jessie brought in the dessert, a sherry trifle topped with strawberries and cream, and Teri saw that she had given Jill's portion, snug in its red plastic dish, an extra dollop of cream. Jill had found a friend, no doubt about that. And the gesture was appreciated, for the little girl attacked the confection with an enthusiasm which she had not extended to the rest of the meal.

Teri herself took just a spoonful, then let it stand. What little appetite she had had was now gone.

'No taste for trifle?' she heard Sloan ask.

Did he watch her every move? Analyse her constantly?

She shook her head and made a disarmingly rueful mouth. 'It's delicious, but I can't manage any more.'

'I'm disappointed. I had you marked as a girl who would enjoy a good trifle.' His voice was bland, but his eyes glinted with mischief.

A private joke. One that only you and I understand, Teri thought. The sort of thing lovers delight in.

But we are *not* lovers! Even though I let myself be carried away today, and for a few seconds showed you just how much you could stir me. You *do* stir me, Sloan, I've been aware of you from the moment I came into this room, I can't fool myself on that score. But I don't love you. I don't even like you. And you've made it clear you don't like me.

'Sorry to disappoint you,' she said lightly.

'Unpredictable, are you?'

'I would hope so.' She darted him a flirtatious smile from beneath her long lashes. 'Predictability makes life boring, don't you think?'

Emma gave a soft laugh, and Virginia said, 'After dinner you must tell me what you've been up to since I last saw you, Sloan.'

Once again the subject was being deftly changed. Virginia did not want Sloan's attentions centred on Teri, and in a sense the girl was relieved. It was hard enough to spar with Sloan when they were alone together. In company she found it even harder. Was Virginia attracted to him? A foolish question. Painfully she acknowledged that most women would be attracted to Sloan. She wondered if Virginia was aware of the fact that there was a Miranda, that she had competition.

'You'll have to catch up on news another time,' said Emma. 'After dinner I would like you all to join me in the library.'

Absorbed as she was in her own thoughts, Teri caught the serious inflection in her friend's tone. There really is an undercurrent, she thought with a sudden quiver of apprehension. And it's leading somewhere. And I'm not sure I want to be around when it reaches its destination.

The library was a lovely room. Panelled in a warm red-brown mahogany, two of its walls were lined with books. The third wall was all glass, but it was dark now, and the curtains had been drawn across the big French windows. The remaining wall had a fireplace, and the air was just chill enough for a fire to have been lit.

Dinner over, Teri had taken Jill to bed, but Emma had insisted that she come to the library once the little girl was settled. Joining the others, she found them ranged around the fire, liqueur glasses in hand.

There was conversation, but it was of a desultory kind. Virginia was flirting with Sloan, but she and Bruce exchanged occasional glances.

Then Emma said, 'My dears,' and there was a sudden hush. It was as if they had all been waiting for her to speak.

'My dears,' she said again, 'I think you know I had a purpose in asking you all to be with me tonight.' She took a sip from her glass, and the silence in the room was intense.

'Bruce asked me why I came back to Vins Doux,' she went on. 'I said it was time. That it was home. And so it is.'

There was an infinitesimal pause as she looked at Sloan, and Teri knew, quite certainly, that Sloan had persuaded her to come back. Whatever Emma had told her to the contrary.

'The reason I left here is personal. I was looking for something, and I think I found it. But Vins Doux is home, I know that now.'

Teri felt a lump rise in her throat. She had never heard Emma quite so serious, with the words seeming to come from her heart. The attention of the others was also riveted on the elderly woman.

'I know too that I won't be here always. In recent months I have been giving a great deal of thought to the estate, and to what will happen to it. My beloved Roger is no longer with me, and I don't have children. You, my dear Virginia and Bruce, are my only relatives.'

If it was possible for the silence to have become more concentrated, then this had now happened. An ember stirred in the fire, and the crackle sounded as loud as a rifle-shot.

'My doctor assures me that I'm in fine health and likely to be here a long time,' Emma went on. 'But I don't want the people closest to me to wait to come into their inheritance. I want them to enjoy it now.' She smiled. 'That way I can share in their enjoyment.'

'I don't want to be rude, Aunt Emma,' Virginia said silkily. 'But perhaps Teri should be excused from this ... from a family discussion.'

The merest flicker of annoyance crossed Emma's face, but it was quickly erased. 'On the contrary,' she countered firmly, 'what I have to say concerns Teri as much as it does the rest of you.'

The apprehension that had been with Teri all evening quickened. A little hammer began to pound in her head. She wanted nothing so much as to leave the room, to take a walk outside in the cool night air.

Emma spread her hands. 'I want the four of you to have Vins Doux now, and in equal shares.'

There was an instant buzz of noise. Teri gave a small incredulous gasp, and heard Bruce exclaim.

Emma gestured, and they quietened. 'I shall continue living here. Obviously it will be my home for as long as I want it.'

'This is very generous of you, Aunt Emma.' Bruce looked a little stunned.

Virginia came to her feet and kissed her aunt on the cheek, and said, 'That's fantastic!'

Teri said nothing. She couldn't have spoken, not now. Now when she felt as if she was in a dream, as if she must waken at any moment.

Sloan did not speak either. She looked across at him. His eyes held hers steadily, and she saw that they were sardonic. His lips were firmly set, and his jaw was a cruel line.

Teri felt a trembling seize her, and she had to curl her fingers hard into the palms of her hands, letting the nails bite into the soft flesh to prevent the trembling from becoming visible.

Emma, as if she was unaware of the tension she had caused, was talking once more. 'Of course there are certain legal procedures—I won't go into the details now. But there is just one thing I must mention.' She looked from one to the other. 'Though I want you all to think of Vins Doux as yours, you will only receive legal ownership a year from now.'

Bruce looked at her puzzled. 'A kind of probation?'

'In a sense. I want you to spend as much time here as you can. And for each of you there will also be a special project.'

'Project?' This from Virginia.

'We'll go into all that tomorrow.' Emma smiled as she stood up and went to a trolley on which stood a tray with glasses and a bottle in an ice-bucket. 'This moment calls for champagne. Sloan, would you help me please?'

This isn't happening, Teri thought, as she watched Sloan uncork the bottle. I'm dreaming, I must be. But if I'm not, if I'm awake, why did Sloan look quite so angry?

Emma poured the champagne, and then they were all standing, clinking glasses, wishing each other good luck in what would be their mutual endeavours.

It was only when the excitement had died a little that Virginia voiced the question that had been on Teri's mind since Emma's announcement. 'Why did you include Teri, Aunt Emma?'

'Because it's what she deserves.'

Virginia's face went red, but she persisted nevertheless. 'She's your companion!'

Only a companion, the tone seemed to suggest. Paid to perform her duties, few as they are.

'She's more than a companion,' Emma corrected. 'She's a friend. A very dear friend.'

Her tone was pleasant, yet firm. Even Virginia knew better than to take the subject further.

It was a restless girl who tossed and turned between

the sheets that night. She had convinced herself, finally, that she was not dreaming. That Emma had meant what she'd said. Teri was really to have a share of Vins Doux.

It was wonderful. Incredible. Beyond any fantasy she could ever have dreamed up.

It was also impossible.

Minute by minute the reality of the situation became clearer to her. It was one thing to live on the wine estate as Emma's companion. It would be quite another to be one of the owners, having to cope with the resentment of Virginia and Bruce, a resentment that was inevitable, for as Emma's relatives they would not feel that an outsider was entitled to a share of Vins Doux.

The hardest thing of all would be the fact that Sloan would be here. Sloan, with his arrogance and contempt. Sloan, who could excite Teri with a touch, who could disturb her with the mere fact of his presence in the same room.

The solution came to her suddenly. It was so simple that she wondered why she had not thought of it sooner. Sleep came at last.

In spite of her disturbed night, Teri woke at dawn. Jill was already chattering to her doll in the adjoining room, and she greeted Teri with a bright smile and the hug of two warm arms around her neck.

'I'm going to dress you, honey,' Teri told her, 'and then we'll go outside. But it's very early, and everyone is asleep, so we'll have to be quiet.'

On tiptoe they stole out of the house, Jill with rubber Miffi—her inseparable companion—held tightly in one hand. In the garden the shrubs were still webbed with dew, and the ground was wet underfoot. The air was crisp and sweet-smelling and Teri was glad that she had dressed Jill warmly.

They walked a little way, stopping once to watch

some birds calling to each other in a tree; a few minutes later to see a centipede trail its many-footed way across the path. A butterfly hovered over the grass, and Teri stood smiling as a rapturous Jill darted hither and thither behind the brightly-coloured insect.

Where the garden gave way to the vineyards they stopped and turned. It was too early to walk here, for the vines hung heavy and wet over the narrow path and Jill would get soaked.

The house was before them as they began to walk back. Brooding, mysterious in the light of early morning. Shuttered and closed still, yet on the threshold of a new day.

A new era, Teri thought. The first day on which four people would begin to think of Vins Doux in a different way. With pride, with interest. With love. Its foundations laid almost two hundred years earlier, Vins Doux had a remarkable history, a new chapter of which was about to unfold.

Four people—Bruce and Virginia; Sloan; Teri. Each would add to the history of the lovely wine estate in his or her own way. Teri felt a lump rise in her throat, and she blinked away sudden tears.

Realisation came suddenly. Four people? What on earth was she thinking about? Last night she had made a decision, and she meant to abide by it. Taking Jill by the hand, she walked back the way she had come, and tried to keep her eyes away from the beautiful house.

'What a delicious thought!' Emma Roland was smiling as she took the steaming cup from Teri. 'Coffee in bed—a nice luxury for an old lady!'

'You're not an old lady, and you know it.' Teri smiled affectionately back at her. 'May I stay while you drink it?'

'You know you may. Sit down, Teri, and tell me what's bothering you.' She chuckled as the girl looked at her startled. 'You came in here with anxiety written all over your face.'

'I did want to catch you before you join the others for breakfast,' Teri admitted ruefully.

She took a sip of her own coffee. Now that she was here, it was surprisingly difficult to get the words out.

'Why not start at the beginning?' Emma suggested.

Teri gave a shaky laugh. 'You're a fairy godmother, perceptive and shrewd and handing out all sorts of lovely temptations. All right, Emma, I'll start at the beginning. I'll say what I should have said last night, which is thank you. I couldn't say it then, I'm sorry.'

'You were in a state of shock.'

'Yes, I was. Emma, I do thank you, from the very bottom of my heart. It was a wonderful thing to do for me. *Too* wonderful. . . .' She looked up, and green eyes were troubled. 'I can't accept it.'

'Why not?'

'I feel I'm not entitled to it.'

'And there you're wrong.'

'Virginia and Bruce are your family.'

Sloan, of course was not, but she couldn't mention him. It was very hard to speak Sloan's name with any degree of naturalness.

'Virginia and Bruce are my sister's children. I love them very dearly, more so perhaps because I never had children of my own. But I'm not blind, Teri, I'm aware of their shortcomings.'

'You don't have to tell me this,' Teri said gently.

'I won't go into details. But I will say this—for much of my life, Teri, people have given me friendship and respect because I was Emma Roland. Because I had money and status.'

'No.' Teri shook her head. 'They like you because of what you are. Warm and friendly and compassionate.' She stopped suddenly. 'So that's why you left Vins Doux. . . .'

'And now *you* are perceptive.' Grey eyes were warm. 'I had a great need to live incognito, to see if I could make it on my own. Can you understand that?'

'Yes,' said Teri after a moment, wonderingly.

'I had a wonderful time in Johannesburg. Not always easy, but pretty wonderful. I found out things about myself that I had never known. Things about people.' Once more she smiled. 'I could go on at length, but right now I want to talk about you. You helped an elderly lady who'd turned her ankle in a supermarket.'

'It was what anybody would have done,' Teri said awkwardly.

'Not the people I've known till now, my dear. You did more than help me that day. You befriended me. You did my shopping, and brought me library books. You visited me when your own time was at a premium. You've no idea how you and Jill cheered me up when I was immobile.'

'Emma——' Teri began, but the other woman silenced her with a gesture.

'You did it all because you wanted to. Without any thought for yourself or for my position—you didn't know that I had one. You have some qualities, my dear, that are increasingly rare in today's world.'

'I'm very ordinary,' Teri protested.

'Not in my eyes. I want you to have a share in Vins Doux, Teri.'

'It doesn't seem right somehow.' She stopped. And then, 'Is Sloan special to you?' Until the moment the question was out she had not known she would ask it.

'Very special. Sloan Garfield is one of the finest people I know.' Grey eyes were steady, as if they were trying to tell her something beyond the words Emma had spoken. Teri found she could not sustain the gaze, and she looked away.

'I can't accept my share,' she said unsteadily.

'I thought my reasons for giving it to you are now clear.'

'They are—oh, they are. Emma, don't press me.' Teri's head was throbbing. She had not thought this would be so difficult. 'I can't explain,' she went on after a moment. 'Emma . . . I think perhaps I should leave here.'

'No.' The older woman's voice was firm. 'I won't hear of it. You made a commitment, and I want you to stay.'

'You don't understand. . . .' Teri's tone was tinged with despair.

'Perhaps I do.' It was said gently. 'Let's make a bargain. Don't tell the others that you've declined your share. Give yourself time to think. A year, Teri, that's all I ask of you.'

A year. Such a short time in the frame of a lifetime. A year for Jill to revel in the sun and sand of the Cape, in the good food and luxuriousness of Vins Doux.

A year in Sloan's presence. Could Teri live through it and emerge with peace of mind and heart intact?

'There's so little for me to do here,' she said at length. 'It's not as if you need someone to take care of you.'

'That's true. Last night I spoke of projects. I'll tell you now what I have in mind for you, Teri.'

A history of Vins Doux. The librarian in Teri thrilled with excitement as Emma spoke. The history of Vins Doux was long and complicated and interwoven with the history of the Cape. But the written word was fragmented; it had never been set down in one piece before.

'It's a project that's very dear to my heart,' Emma

said. It was also one that would take months to research before pen could be put to paper.

'Think you'd enjoy it?' Emma asked at length.

'I'd love it,' Teri said softly.

'And you will stay?'

'Yes.'

Teri was in the garden with Jill when Jessie came outside and asked if she could play with the child. With the library on her mind, Teri was happy to say yes.

The room was even more beautiful than she had realised. Till now she had obtained no more than an impression of it. Now, alone, able to walk around the book-lined walls, she was fascinated. She had not dreamed that such a wealth of books could be in a private collection.

Librarianship was more than an occupation for Teri. She loved books with a passion. Reverently she touched pages that were a hundred years old or more, wondering as she did so about the generations of people who had read them and touched them in years gone by.

There were books of all kinds. Biographies, history, tales of exploration. Fiction both classic and modern. Books on wine-making. Books on the history of the Cape.

Like Jill in the toy department, Teri did not know where to look first. She wanted to see everything, read everything, and knew she could spend years in this room and not see all of it.

'I'm hooked,' she said aloud, joyously. 'You knew I would be, Emma, you clever woman!'

She knew where she would start. The history of the Cape was as much a part of the story of Vins Doux as was wine-making. Some of it she knew already, it was time to refresh her memory.

She was standing at the bay window, attention riveted on a tale of the past, when someone queried, 'Interesting book?'

'Oh Sloan, yes! A story about a woman called Anna Deltjie. The most fascinating woman. Do you know about her?'

In the elfin-shaped face, green eyes were shining. Like emeralds, thought the man.

'A familiar name,' he said dryly.

'Silly question.' She smiled up at him. 'You read biography, you *would* know about her. What a character, Sloan!'

'Not unlike you.' He said it softly.

'Me?' The smile left her face as something in his face made her take a step away from him. As usual he was casually dressed, a fawn tee-shirt showing every muscle of his chest and shoulders, the corduroy trousers revealing the tautness of his legs. Virility was proclaimed in every long inch of him.

'Don't you recognise yourself in Anna?' He was smiling, but there was no amusement in the blue eyes, and the lips were sardonic.

'No.' For some reason the joy was suddenly gone. 'Should I?'

'Anna was unscrupulous, but she got away with it because she was a woman of great charm,' he said, and now his tone was definitely dangerous. 'It was said that she could charm the birds from the trees. Do you think, like you, she could also make them sing to her tune?'

CHAPTER SEVEN

THE colour drained from Teri's cheeks. 'How dare you, Sloan! You're suggesting I conned Emma. . . .'

'She was also very sexy,' he went on, as if he had not heard a word that she had said.

Heart beginning to pound, she stared at him. Sexy? Sloan thought she was sexy? 'About Emma, you don't understand. . . .'

'And beautiful.'

'Beautiful.' Anger at his insinuations was submerged in the greater amazement at his compliments. 'Sloan, I'm not sexy and beautiful.' And then more doubtfully, 'Am I?'

'Don't you know?'

It took him just seconds to cross the small space between them. There was no time for her to move away, and short of jumping out of the window, no place for her to escape. Even then, a part of her knew that she did not want to escape.

He drew her to him, hands closing on her shoulders before sliding sensuously down her back to her waist. For a long moment he stood quite still, looking down at her, and he was so near to her that she could see each tiny dark speck in the blue of his eyes.

'Sloan?' On a dry throat the name came out on a whisper.

'You want me to kiss you, is that it, Teri?'

She shook her head. 'Am I really beautiful . . . and sexy?'

'I'll prove it to you.'

His mouth touched hers gently, tantalisingly. With

the tip of his tongue he trailed a path around her lips, circling them before moving to her eyes and her cheeks, and then down to her throat. Last time he had kissed her there had been roughness, anger. This kiss was different, undermining her resistance and making her feel weak. Even before his hands slid to her hips, drawing her closer against him, she felt desire stir within her.

By the time his lips rose in search of hers again her own response was unthinking, instinctive, and her mouth opened willingly beneath his as she returned kiss for kiss.

Her body was filled with an excitement that grew minute by minute as his hands began to move over her, from her hips back to her waist, over her stomach and then up to her breasts. She was barely aware of the fingers that went to the buttons of her shirt, and later she knew she could not have stopped him. He was kissing her deeply now, his mouth never leaving hers, and as she felt his hand on the bare skin of her breasts a moan emerged from her throat. Mindlessly she wound her arms around his neck, pressing herself closer against him, letting her own fingers bury themselves in the thickness of his hair.

It was Sloan who broke contact first. His head lifted and he looked down at her, and beneath his tan he was a little pale.

'You *are* sexy,' he murmured huskily.

Only for you, she wanted to say. I've never felt this way with any man before. Never imagined I could respond like this. She was about to put something of her feelings into words, mindless at that moment of how Sloan would construe them, when he added, 'Like Anna.'

'Anna?' She stared at him uncomprehendingly.

'Sexy and beautiful.'

There had been more to the description. 'And unscrupulous,' she said dully.

His eyes held hers a moment, then went to the lips he had just kissed. 'Right now sex and beauty was all I had on my mind.'

She pushed herself a little away from him. 'But you do think I'm unscrupulous?'

'You talk too much. Come here, Teri.'

He wanted to kiss her again. And she wanted him to, God, how she wanted him to! But not in the circumstances.

'Let me go, Sloan,' she muttered.

'You're enjoying this.' His voice roughened a little. 'We're both enjoying it. You can't deny it. Not after the way you respond.'

'I don't deny that you excite me, how can I?' The words came out painfully. 'But there has to be trust before there can be. . . .' She stopped, appalled, for the word that had so nearly emerged from her lips was 'love'. 'Before there can be kissing,' she went on shakily.

He did not answer immediately. Instead his hands went once more to her hips, drawing her to him. Expert hands, sensuous, able to seduce a girl with the merest touch of long fingers. Teri's legs felt like water.

'I'll show you how wrong you are,' he murmured softly as his head came down.

In the moment before his searching mouth could find hers, she summoned the strength to twist her head away.

'You *don't* trust me,' she insisted. 'You really think I conned Emma.'

'My thoughts are my own.' His voice was hard.

'You think I conned her into giving me a share of Vins Doux.'

'Did you?'

What would you say if I told you that I'd declined my share? Would that take the insolent drawl from your tone and the sardonic look that I hate so much from your face?

'Did you?' he asked again.

Even if I hadn't given Emma a promise I wouldn't tell you the truth, Teri thought. Trust has to be given freely. That's how I want it from you.

'You must believe what you want,' she said with a lightness she was far from feeling.

'What I want to believe and what I know are two different things.' His tone was angry, and the fingers on her waist bit into her with sudden cruelty. 'I look at you and I see the face of an angel. Beautiful, innocent. And I know that you're not innocent at all.'

'Get out of here!' Her voice shook.

A hand went to her breasts. With the tantalising lightness that was so devastating, it stroked a path around one breast, then the other, then caught a nipple between long fingers. Teri closed her eyes, willing herself to banish the sweetness that was like agony inside her. She could not let herself give in to sensations that threatened to overwhelm her. She could *not*, for if she did she was lost.

'Don't,' she muttered through clenched teeth.

'You know you want it.' His voice was surprisingly rugged as a nipple hardened between his fingers. 'Your body gives you away.'

She did know it, and the knowledge was painful. 'Yes,' she said, opening her eyes and forcing herself to meet his. 'But not like this. Not without your trust.'

'Don't make the terms impossible,' he whispered. 'We have something good going for us, Teri.'

The other hand began to trail a path along her throat, and then he kissed her again. Sensuously drugging kisses, kisses that undermined her resolve and coaxed a response from her.

It was hard to think rationally when her mind and body were filled with the delight of what was happening. When all she wanted was to surrender to his demands, and to the demands of a need that was like a fire inside her.

Hard, but not impossible. In a corner of her mind some sense still lingered, and it came to her rescue now. 'It's no good,' she said when he paused to draw breath.

'What the hell are you talking about? It's pretty marvellous, and you know it.'

'Not without trust, Sloan.' She didn't think she could push herself from his arms, but somehow she managed it. With hands that shook she began to fasten the buttons of her blouse.

'You're a fool if you confuse trust with sex.' There was a strange expression in his eyes as he watched her fumbling attempts with the buttons.

'Then I must be a fool.'

'You're not a virgin, Teri. Don't behave like one.'

She couldn't look at him. She was going to cry, and she didn't want him here when it happened.

'Get out, Sloan!' Her tone was low and barely audible, pitched to a level where he would not hear the choking lump in her throat. 'Get out, because if you don't I'll press the bell and call for help.'

'Don't bother.' His tone was heavy with scorn. 'I've never had to force myself on a woman yet, I don't intend to start now.'

It was as well that he left when he did, for her reservoir of control was almost exhausted. A shuddering gripped her just moments after the door had closed, leaving her so weak that she sank back against the wall for support. It was a minute or two before she began to feel better. Taking a few deep breaths, she dashed

the tears from her eyes with an angry hand, and
resolved that she would never allow Sloan Garfield to
humiliate her again.

Some semblance of order restored to her appearance,
Teri took the book she had been reading when Sloan
came in and put it back where it belonged. It would be
some time before she felt like learning more about
Anna Deltjie.

Taking two other books from the shelves, she
settled down at a polished walnut desk with a stack of
index cards and a pen. The joy that had been with her
earlier, when she had been fired with the idea of
reading and research, had waned. Yet she was grateful
for the task Emma had given her, for it would
consume hours of her time. In her determination to
avoid Sloan and the need to fill her days, the library
would become a haven and an escape.

Opening one of the books, she began to read. She
had read three pages when she looked up, knowing she
had not taken in a word of it. A second attempt proved
equally futile.

Angrily she got to her feet and went to the window.
Below her a wistaria was a cloud of delicate lilac. The
scent of it would be delicious on the hot still air, but
Teri could not smell it. It was as if Sloan had a
monopoly on her sensations. She could still taste him
on her lips, could feel his hands where he had touched
her. Her nostrils were filled with the clean male smell
of him. The appalling thing, the utterly appalling
thing, was that she did not know how to rid herself of
the sensations.

'Dear God,' she groaned despairingly into the silence
of the book-filled room, 'what am I going to do?'

Teri toyed with the tempting idea of skipping lunch,

then dismissed it reluctantly as foolish. Her absence would reveal to Sloan just how much his lovemaking had affected her. It would give him untold satisfaction, spurring him on perhaps to even more determined efforts.

'I don't want him to touch me again,' she told herself grimly. 'And he has to know that he can't intimidate me.'

In the event, Sloan was not there and Teri was not sure whether to be relieved or sorry. The meal, as with breakfast, was taken buffet-style, and only Bruce was present.

'Teri!' he exclaimed on a note of pleasure, as he turned from the long serving-trolley from which he had been helping himself to food. 'I was just thinking about you.'

'Only nice things, I hope,' she said lightly.

'I don't think there could be anything bad where you're concerned,' he said softly. 'How very pretty you look in that outfit. Green suits your eyes, did you know?'

She smiled bleakly. 'Why, thank you.'

'Help yourself to some lunch and join me. I'm really glad we came in at the same time.' His tone was warm.

The events of the morning had left Teri without any appetite, but she put some chicken on to her plate, as well as small servings of potato salad and cole-slaw.

'So little?' Bruce's eyebrows rose at sight of her plate.

'I'm not very hungry.'

'No wonder you're so slender. Very feminine, though, if you don't mind me saying so.'

Sloan had no care for Teri's reactions to the things he said. The things that he *did*. A picture came into her mind, unbidden—Sloan's hands on her throat and at her breasts. She shivered. If memory alone was

enough to produce sensations she could well do
without, was there any hope for her at Vins Doux?
What am I going to do? she thought again.

'Are you all right?'

Teri came back to her surroundings. With a little
shock of surprise she saw that Bruce was beside her.
He was watching her, his eyes warm with concern. For
a few moments, as long as the memory had been in her
mind, she had actually been unaware of him.

Am I so far gone? she wondered.

'Are you all right?' he asked again.

'Yes, of course.'

'For a moment you had me worried. You looked a
little pale. . . .'

'I'm fine.'

She gave another smile, forcing some brightness this
time. Bruce was no Sloan. He was a caring person, a
nice person. Nice was the adjective she had already
decided could not be used in reference to Sloan. A
moment of insight told her that the tall tanned farmer
would rather be called anything but that.

'Why don't you eat?'

'I will,' she said.

'Has Emma spoken to you about your project?'

'Yes.'

'Tell me about it,' he invited.

Teri looked up from the food that she was pushing
listlessly about with her fork. Bruce met her eyes and
smiled and said, 'Please. . . .' And there was something
appealing in his face, something little-boyish that she
had not noticed before.

She had assessed him wrongly. Last night she had
taken him for a man who was mechanically gallant to all
women, but whose real interest lay in girls of wit and
sophistication. If anything, he had seemed bored with
her. I must have been wrong, she admitted to herself now.

Attentively he listened while she spoke. Careful to make no mention of Anna Deltjie, she told him the few facts she had already discovered about the days of the earliest vineyards.

'That's fascinating,' Bruce exclaimed when Teri lapsed into silence.

'I think so too.'

'I just hope you won't let yourself get too busy, though. I'll be spending quite some time at Vins Doux myself from now on, and I'd like to think we could spend some of it together.'

Fast worker, she thought, sucking in her breath. She had enough complications in her life at this moment, she had no need of more.

Looking up, she saw that he was watching her. As Sloan so often did. But Bruce's eyes lacked the mockery and the hardness she had grown to dread in Sloan's expression. Bruce's eyes were brown and warm, friendly.

She could use a friend. There was Emma, of course. But she could do with a man who liked her for herself, unconditionally.

Her face relaxed. 'I'd like to spend some time with you,' she smiled.

'Good.' A hand reached across the table and covered her fingers. I feel nothing, Teri thought, knowing that Sloan did not have to touch her to excite her. Just his presence in a room was enough. In a way it was good that she did not react to Bruce, she had enough to cope with in the physical area already. In another way it was disastrous. Bruce could well represent Everyman. Every man other than Sloan. But Sloan was not for her, and never could be. Did that mean that she was destined to spend the rest of her life alone?

'Interrupting things, am I?' asked a husky voice.

'No,' Teri answered Virginia with as much dignity as she could, withdrawing her hand at the same time.

'Glad you two are getting along so well.' There was a swift exchange of looks between brother and sister, and then Virginia went on lightly, 'At least some people are having fun.'

'What's eating you, Ginny?' asked Bruce.

'This place. The whole damn set-up.'

'Ginny——' Bruce began warningly.

'Don't shut me up! It's fine for you, brother dear. You'll have to learn a little more about the wine business, but that's no big deal. And you'll have your fun at the same time.' The last words were accompanied with a meaning look at Teri, who flushed with quick anger.

She opened her mouth to retort, but was forestalled by Bruce, who said again warningly, 'Ginny!'

'All right, all right.' Another exchange of looks which Teri was too angry to interpret. 'I've spent the last hour with Aunt Emma. You'll never guess—she expects me to start a day-care facility.'

'A what?' Bruce was mystified.

'A day-care, for God's sake. A place where the farm-workers can leave their children.'

'That sounds a worthwhile project,' Teri said quietly. 'I was strolling through the compound just yesterday, and I wondered about all the little ones whose parents spend their days in the vineyards.'

'Worthwhile be damned! I'm a fashion model, for heaven's sake, not a stupid nanny!'

'You'll have to give up your modelling?' Bruce queried disbelievingly.

'Even Aunt Emma knows better than to ask that of me. She expects me to get the wretched thing started. Someone else will run it, but I'll be expected to supervise. What the hell!'

'We'll talk about this later, Ginny.'

Bruce spoke with a firmness that surprised Teri and obviously impressed his sister, for the latter stiffened a moment before saying, 'Sure.' Then a smile spread over taut features as she added, 'More time at Vins Doux will have its compensations, of course. Can't say I object to seeing more of Sloan. He's some gorgeous hunk, don't you think, Teri?'

'I hadn't noticed,' Teri said through dry lips.

'Oh, come on! He's the sexiest creature in trousers for miles around.'

'There's Miranda,' Bruce said tersely. 'She's still on the scene, I've been told.'

Virginia gave a brittle laugh. 'I wouldn't have thought you'd give me Miranda as a reason to hold back, brother dear. Besides, competition adds spice to life, don't you agree, Teri?'

'I wouldn't know,' Teri answered on a wave of pain.

'And I thought you'd be one who would know these things,' Virginia came back archly.

No mistaking her meaning. As an unmarried mother Teri was presumed to be wise in the ways of the world. How astounded Virginia would be when she learned the truth. How astounded they all would be!

Just then Emma entered the room, sparing Teri the necessity of a comeback. But there would be other remarks, she knew that. Remarks that would hit at Jill's presence in her life. Until she was ready to proclaim the little girl as her sister, she would have to learn to cope with them.

'How nice to find you all here together.' The older woman was smiling.

'I was just telling Bruce and Teri about my project.' Virginia's tone bubbled with an enthusiasm Teri had not heard before. 'So worthwhile. So many little children left alone all day while their parents are working. It will be wonderful for them to have a place where they can be taken care of.'

'I'm glad you feel that way, Virginia,' Emma said quietly, as Teri drew breath. 'Earlier I thought I detected some resentment. I'm so glad I was wrong.'

'Wrong as can be, Aunt Emma. I can't wait to begin. Why, Teri, you're not off already?'

'If you'll excuse me.' Teri glanced at Emma. 'It's later than I thought. Jessie must be wanting her own lunch. I think I should go outside to Jill.'

Teri spent the afternoon in the garden with Jill and Emma. Jill played with the rubber doll, while the other two busied themselves with hooking the wall-hangings. It was quiet in the garden and companionable, and Teri told Emma a little about the reading she had done in the library that morning.

'I think you'll accomplish wonders,' the older woman said.

'I hope so.'

'I know so. Vins Doux will at last have a history future generations can take pride in. Teri dear, I don't want to dwell on the issue—but remember your promise, will you?' And as the girl looked up, green eyes troubled, 'You will stay here a year, and you'll tell nobody that you've refused your share.'

A promise which, on the surface of it, should not be difficult to keep, Teri reflected a while later, as she walked alone through the gardens. She and Jill could not have more in the way of creature comforts, and Emma was a gem of an employer.

It was twilight. The sun lit the sky in a blaze of vermilion glory, and a hush lay over the valley and the mountains. From the direction of the compound came the aroma of woodsmoke and roasting meat. In the distance a dog barked, then was still. It was all so beautiful, Teri thought, pausing to drink in the loveliness all around her.

The undercurrents she sensed at Vins Doux seemed at this moment to exist in another world. Pity Sloan was not in that world with them. He was in her mind, in her senses. Every feature of his face was crystal clear, as were his voice and his gestures, the taste of his lips and the touch of his hands.

'If only I could find a way not to think of him,' she murmured to herself. 'I *have* to find a way. . . .'

'Talking to yourself?' a laughing voice questioned, and spinning round Teri saw Bruce. 'What were you saying?' he wanted to know.

'Something to the effect that it's all so beautiful,' she lied. She made a wide gesture. 'I've never seen anything quite like it.'

'It is beautiful,' he agreed. 'Do you know Kirstenbosch, Teri? And Cape Point?'

She smiled. 'Familiar names to me only, I'm afraid.'

'Have to remedy that. I'm going your way, so we may as well walk together.' So saying, he put his arm around her shoulders. For a moment her impulse was to resist the gesture, and then she realised that a gesture was all it was. Affectionate, warm—a little flirtatious perhaps. But Bruce was her friend, and she needed a friend. She made no effort to move away from him.

'Some day I'm going to show you all there is to see in the Cape,' he was saying. 'There's so much. . . .'

He stopped as a figure came into sight, tall and lean, with a face that was tanned and hard. There was a bleak expression on that face, and the sensuous lips were set in a cruel line. Sloan was angry, Teri saw in a flash, and wondered why.

All three had stopped quite still in their tracks. Bruce chose the moment to draw Teri closer against him, sliding his hand along her arm. A provocative gesture, and one that was not lost on Sloan, for his eyebrows rose mockingly. Curtly he nodded to them, then walked on.

'Arrogant bastard,' Bruce muttered.

At any other time Teri might have agreed with him, but now her throat was dry, and there were no words that came to her lips.

'Glad you came?'

'Mm,' Teri murmured on a sigh of pleasure. The beach-sand was soft and warm beneath her thighs and her toes and the skin of her midriff where it was left bare by the bikini. The crash of waves was a sound of which she never tired, and the sun was just pleasantly hot. She could feel the warmth on her back, her skin seemed to be soaking it in. It was a wonderful feeling.

'Better than spending the day doing research?'

'Fantastic. I missed my vocation. I should have been a beachcomber. Oh, Bruce, this is the life!'

He laughed. 'Beachcombers look better without stripes on their backs. Why don't you undo the clasp of your bikini top?'

Why not indeed? Her favourite sun-dress plunged deeply at the back, and the white stripes the bikini would leave on her skin after a day in the sun would mar its effect. while she lay face downwards on the sand her breasts would not be seen. Besides, this was such a lonely strip of beach, almost private.

'Let me,' said Bruce, and without waiting for her consent he unclasped the bikini and pushed down the straps. Then he let his hand rest on the bare skin of her back, before sliding it down to her hips. 'I feel nothing,' Teri said to herself not for the first time. 'Absolutely nothing.'

'Don't,' she said quietly.

'Couldn't resist it, honey.'

'Jill's here. I don't want her to see. . . .'

An excuse. Jill was busy making a sand-castle, and even if she had noticed what Bruce did, the little girl was too young to know that the touch of a man's hand could be suggestive. I don't enjoy being touched by Bruce, Teri thought.

She ached with sudden longing as a picture of Sloan came into her mind. She lay very still. In the distance there was the sound of voices, but they made no impression on her. 'I must stop thinking of Sloan,' she told herself fiercely. I can't control my dreams at night, but I must try to think of other things when I'm awake.'

'You'll burn,' said Bruce, as the voices grew louder.

'I do need some suntan lotion,' Teri conceded. She had oiled Jill well, but for some reason had neglected herself. Reaching behind her, she made to refasten the clasp of her top prior to sitting up.

Bruce forestalled her. 'Let me. Jill won't be corrupted by this.'

Dropping a little oil on her back, he began to rub it in. Teri lay still, her head averted, and wished the hand belonged to Sloan. Wished thus despite her resolve not to think of him again.

The voices grew louder. Women's voices. And then a laugh, a man's laugh, low and husky and seductive. Teri would have known that laugh anywhere. Her stomach muscles contracted in sudden alarm.

'Bruce!' Virginia's voice. 'Had you given up on us?'

'Not quite,' he called back.

'Sloan and Virginia? You knew they were coming?' Teri twisted her head to look at Bruce, who was bending over her lazily, rubbing the oil into her back. Her breathing was shaky, and her eyes and her mouth felt stiff.

'Of course I knew. Miranda's with them.'

Teri's muscles were so tight now that breathing was painful. 'Why didn't you tell me?'

'I suppose I didn't think of it,' Bruce said blandly.

He was lying. He'd kept the knowledge from her deliberately. But why?

The question fled her mind as a pair of legs suddenly filled her vision. Powerful legs with well-shaped feet and muscled calves, so close to her that she could see the dark hairs curling on the tanned skin. Fascinated, her eyes lifted, and now she could see Sloan's long thighs, and the narrow hips encased in white swimming trunks. Slowly, involuntarily almost, her eyes went further, to the trim waist and the broad chest, coming to rest at length on a face that was tanned and ruggedly chiselled with a jawline that was relentlessly grim.

He was all male, she thought, on a surge of primeval pleasure. Male in a way that she had never encountered before. He was also the picture of displeasure.

'Hello, Sloan,' she managed on a jerky indrawn breath.

'Hello, Teri.' His tone was as grim as his face.

The reason for his attitude came to her suddenly. In the last minutes she had been oblivious of the open bikini top, of Bruce rubbing oil into her back. So indifferent was she to the younger man that the situation had meant almost nothing to her. She had been conscious only of Sloan's approach. Now, looking at the scene with Sloan's eyes, she recognised its sexual overtones for the first time.

An explanation tumbled on her tongue, and she opened her mouth to speak—only to close it firmly. No matter the sensations Sloan aroused in her, she owed him nothing in the way of apologies, excuses, or explanations.

'That's enough,' she said quietly to Bruce. With all the dignity she could summon she reached behind her, fastened the clasp of her bikini top, and sat up.

CHAPTER EIGHT

'Teri, I don't believe you've met Miranda.' Virginia made the introductions as she put her towels and bags on the sand.

'Glad to meet you, Teri,' said Miranda with a cold smile. 'Darling,' to Sloan, 'hold the towel straight while I lie down. You know how I hate to get sand all over me.'

She was beautiful, Teri thought numbly. Tall, with her auburn hair coiled in a sophisticated chignon, and with a figure that matched the perfection of her face, Miranda had as much the look of a model as had Virginia.

Somewhere in the inner recesses of Teri's mind there had been the unacknowledged hope that she might compete with Miranda. The unseen Miranda, she had thought of her in the past. Well, she was unseen no longer. I'm no competition for her, Teri decided. Not for Miranda, not for Virginia.

She shifted on her towel, and flinched as she came in contact with a man's hard thighs and chest. Bruce. In her confusion, she had not noticed that he had positioned himself so closely behind her. Her first impulse was to move away. And then she met Sloan's eyes, and their expression was more grim than ever. Grim and contemptuous.

An expression which stirred her to defiance each time she saw it. Sending a provocative smile Sloan's way, she moved an inch nearer to Bruce, and had to stop herself flinching again as she felt his arms close around her waist. 'Nice,' he murmured in her ear, yet just loud enough for the others to hear. 'Very nice!'

Teri saw a muscle move in Sloan's jaw, as Miranda remarked, 'I'd no idea Emma had taken on such an attractive companion.'

'Not only attractive.' Virginia gave her brittle laugh. 'Teri has winning ways too.'

'She does?'

'Didn't you know that Aunt Emma has given Teri an equal share of Vins Doux?'

'Darling, you didn't tell me.' Miranda looked reproachfully at Sloan, and then, with new interest, at Teri. 'Winning ways with men too, it seems, if the little scene we interrupted when we came down is any indication.'

'Why don't we change the subject?' Teri asked restlessly, with a glance at Sloan's furious face. 'I think it's getting a little boring.'

'I'm not bored, honey.' Bruce's breath fanned her ear. 'I can confirm your winning ways with men.'

'Has Teri won you over too, Sloan?' Miranda's voice was husky.

Copper-tanned shoulders gave a dismissive shrug. 'It's you I brought to the beach, remember?'

'So you did.' As Miranda laughed, the tone not unlike Virginia's, she looked at Teri, and there seemed to be a warning in her eyes. Sloan is not for the taking—remember that.

'Why, Miranda,' Virginia said lightly, 'don't you think Sloan has enough on his hands with the two of us?'

A gauntlet? One woman's way of telling another that they were in the field for the same man? Teri stared at Virginia, amazed at the blatancy of the remark. But Miranda, it seemed, was a woman who could handle it. Her responding smile was radiant as she said, 'Ah, but Sloan has the virility of two men. Don't you, my darling?'

They're rivals, Teri thought, dazed, and in some strange way that I can't begin to conceive they are also friends. Perhaps it's because they understand each other.

'What it is to be desired by two females!' Bruce chuckled as he bent forward and dropped a kiss on Teri's ear. 'For myself, I find one woman more than enough.'

This time Teri was unable to quell the shiver of repulsion. From behind her came the hiss of Bruce's indrawn breath, and she felt him tighten. Her reaction had not escaped him.

She had been aware of undercurrents at Vins Doux, and here on the beach there were different ones. She understood them, but only dimly. She was out of her orbit, out of her league. She looked at Sloan.

His eyes met hers steadily. And then he moved his gaze deliberately, from her eyes to her mouth, and then to her throat and to the swell of her breasts. There his eyes seemed to linger a moment, before travelling to the slim stomach and shapely thighs. Teri's bikini was not as revealing as those worn by the other two girls, and yet she felt undressed and humiliated.

Damn you, Sloan! The words thundered in her head, so loudly that it seemed as if the others must hear them. And damn you too, Bruce!

Pushing herself away from Bruce, she got to her feet.

'Honey, where are you going?' she heard him ask.

Anywhere! I have no idea. I just want to be alone. Away from you and Virginia and Miranda, from a game which I don't like or understand. Away from Sloan who humiliates me and looks at me with contempt.

'I'm off for a swim,' she said, amazed that her voice sounded so natural.

'Might be cold, honey.'

She smiled. 'I'm warm-blooded.'

The water *was* cold. It was also wonderful, exhilarating. A wave rose and fell against her hips, and she laughed aloud as the water splashed her. Already she felt better. Turning, she saw the group she had left on the beach. They looked so far away, so small, so unimportant. She should have left them earlier.

She went further. A wave was rising, and she took it in a clean dive. The ocean soared and dipped, and she lay back and let the water carry her. The sky was a metallic blue, with a glare that hurt her eyes, so she closed them. Dipping, soaring, body weightless on the rhythmic swell, Teri felt lulled, totally relaxed.

She did not know which came first, the hand that touched her back or the voice that exclaimed, 'Little fool!' Gasping, she made to stand, and found that her feet did not touch ground.

'You *are* out of your depth.' Sloan's hand was still at her back, and he was so close to her that she saw the drops of water glistening on the hairs of his chest.

His eyes were a deeper blue than the sky, and the lashes were long and fair. His lips were slightly tilted, his teeth white and strong against his tan. The sexual aura that was with him at all times was even more potent now, when his body was wet and the fair damp hair was burnished by the sun. He looked like a pirate, a pirate who pillaged the heart of every girl he encountered.

Oh yes, she was out of her depth. And in more than one way.

Aloud, she said, 'I'm a good swimmer.'

He laughed as his arm passed from behind her forwards in one swift movement. 'Glad to hear it. Start swimming.'

'I intend to and you won't. . . .' The words choked in her throat. 'My bikini!' she exclaimed.

'Yes?' A mocking drawl.

'You've taken my bikini top!' She stared at him disbelievingly as she trod water.

'I saved it.' White teeth glinted wickedly as he waved the tiny piece of emerald cloth he held in his hand. 'If it weren't for me, this tantalising scrap of nothing would be half-way to China by now, sea-nymph!'

Sea-nymph. It had the sound of an endearment. And now she really was imagining things.

'You saved it?'

'I'm holding it, am I not?'

So bemused had Teri been by his unexpected arrival on the scene that he could have unfastened the clasp without her noticing it. But even Sloan would not do such a thing. Would he?

'Give it back to me!'

'In a moment.'

She was acutely aware of her nakedness. The water swirled and crashed around her, and she felt it strong on her nipples. It was an amazing sensation, incredibly sensuous. She was glad that Sloan did not know how she felt, relieved that he could not see her body beneath the water.

'Give it to me now!'

'We'll talk first.'

'Talk! Are you crazy?' She lunged for her bikini and watched enraged as a long arm lifted, taking the garment out of her reach. 'We've nothing to talk about. Sloan, you can't do this to me!'

He laughed, and even over the sound of the waves she could hear the husky seductiveness. It was fire to nerves that were already maddened.

He was teasing her, and he was enjoying it. As she

was enjoying it, she acknowledged shamelessly to herself after a moment of startled self-revelation. But she would not let him know it, and she would not play along with him. She would make a grab for the bikini when she could catch him off guard.

She forced herself to go limp. 'What do you want to talk about?'

'Bruce.'

He *was* crazy. He was also sexier than she had ever thought it possible a man could be.

'Ah, Bruce.' She smiled. 'He's a nice person, Sloan.'

'Nice!' Blue eyes shot sparks of steel, and the laughing mouth was suddenly grim again.

She'd said the wrong thing. The time to catch him off his guard was now, before he became even angrier.

Treading water quickly, she made another lunge towards his hand—which was just out of reach. She had not bargained on his reactions being so swift.

Neither had she realised that the movement would bring her up against him. Her legs were against his, her bare breasts within inches of his chest. She sucked in her breath in shock at the surge of hunger that flamed suddenly through her. For a few moments she could not breathe. Then, recovering some measure of composure, she made to move away from him—and found she could not.

His free arm had gone around her waist and he was holding her to him. Her legs were so weak with longing that she let them lie against his a moment. And then sanity returned, and she looked at him pleadingly.

'Sloan. . . .'

'You want me to make love to you?'

Yes! Oh God, yes! I want you to kiss me and make love to me more than I've ever wanted anything in my life.

'Of course not!'

'Ah,' he said, so lazily that she was unprepared for the head that came down suddenly, for the tongue that traced an experimental line around the shape of her mouth.

Desire was a tangible thing, a pain, gnawing at her, so that she had to close her eyes lest he see the hunger in them.

'I think,' he said, 'that I don't believe you.'

'Sloan. . . .'

'You do want me to make love to you.'

'No!'

'You're angry that I kissed you?'

Was it possible to feel anger when a pirate's laughing mouth was so temptingly close to her own?

'Terribly angry,' she whispered. 'Give me my bikini.'

'When we've talked.'

She remembered. 'About Bruce. . . .'

'Nice Bruce, yes.' Another lick of the tongue, around her ear-lobe this time, and then back to her lips, bringing her a taste of salt.

He pulled her closer to him, and she felt her breasts pushed hard against his chest, her nipples teased by the hair that grew there.

'*This* isn't nice,' he said. 'It's delicious.' He lifted her a little, so that her shoulders were exposed, and then his lips slid over the smooth wet skin. 'More than delicious.'

Teri shuddered. 'Let's talk.'

'It's what you'd prefer?' The laughter was chased from his eyes by an expression of bleakness.

'Yes.'

'All right, then.'

She thought he would release her, that he would give her back the bikini, but he did not. Let me keep my sanity, she prayed, as they were buffeted by the waves and she felt his legs move against her.

'About Bruce.' It was not necessary to shout over the sound of the ocean. So close together were they that each could hear what the other was saying, and any words that were drowned out could be lip-read. 'Leave him alone, Teri.'

She stared at him. 'I don't understand.'

'You should. That was an intimate little scene on the beach a few minutes ago.'

Nowhere near as intimate as this one. She laughed. 'You must be kidding!'

'Teri!' His tone was harsh.

A little bewildered now, she said, 'Bruce was putting on some sun-tan lotion, that was all.'

'That's not how it looked.'

'Well, isn't that too bad.' Her voice rose in sudden anger.

'Don't encourage him, Teri,' Sloan ordered.

'Do you think I am?'

'Maybe.' His thighs moved against her, and she knew for a fact that this time there had been no wave to buffet him. 'God knows you're a tempting little witch. And you've had practice.'

The slap on his cheek was loud, even over the waves. Beneath his tan, Sloan looked a little pale. 'Don't ever do that again,' he ordered.

'Then don't accuse me unjustly!'

There was an odd expression in the eyes that were just inches away from her own. One Teri could not explain. Excitement quivered down her spine.

'You're very beautiful,' Sloan observed at length, his tone ragged. And then, voice hardening, 'So beautiful that I could almost believe Bruce isn't just out for what he can get.'

For a moment the idea that Sloan thought her

beautiful was uppermost in her mind. It was a few seconds before the rest of the statement made an impact, and Teri said, 'What on earth are you talking about?'

'You don't know?'

'What is there to know?'

'If Bruce marries you, between the two of you, you would own a hefty piece of Vins Doux.'

She looked at him, her eyes wide and confused. 'The last thing on my mind is marriage. Heavens, Sloan, Bruce is my friend! He'd be as amazed as I am if he knew what you were saying.'

'There's never been any love lost between Bruce and myself. It would suit him just fine to have eventual control of Vins Doux,' Sloan assured her.

They couldn't be talking business. Not here, like this! With water swirling about them, and her bare breasts brushing his chest. I don't believe it, Teri thought, I don't believe this is happening.

There was another thought too. Sloan hadn't followed her into the water because he wanted to be with her, because she stirred him in the way he stirred her. He was thinking solely of Vins Doux, of a way to protect his own interests.

'You took off my bikini,' she said suddenly.

'What the hell has that got to do with anything?'

'You said you'd rescued it.' Tears stung her eyes, and she was determined that he would not see them. 'You took it off, deliberately, to keep me hostage.'

'And got a lot more than I bargained for.' The skin was stretched taut over the bronzed and rugged cheekbones, and the eyes were blue steel as they stared down at her—almost as if he could make out the contours of her body through the water. 'You're incredibly beautiful.' He sounded suddenly husky.

As he pulled her closer, she could feel his heart

beating against her chest, thudding in unison with her
own. In other circumstances these moments would
have been special, a precious scene that would remain
in her memory as something lovely and exciting. But
Sloan, for purposes of his own, had tricked her into
this situation. And that was not to be borne.

She managed to push herself a little away from him.
'We were talking about Bruce.'

His lips tightened. 'I want you to keep away from
him.'

How dare you order me around! Sloan Garfield. You
are the most dynamic man I've ever met, and my heart
does strange things when I'm near you, but none of
that gives you the right to tell me how to live my life.

'I'll see Bruce whenever I want to,' she told him,
lifting her chin.

He was so close to her that she could feel his chest
move as he drew breath. 'What is it you want from
him? Sex?'

'Why not?' she responded saucily.

'I'll show you why not.' His tone lost its harshness
and became a lazy drawl. 'I can give you all the sex
you want, sea-nymph.'

She knew what was coming, and she grew very still.
There was fear within her, but there was also an
enormous excitement, so that even if she had wanted
to get away from him her treacherous body would
have stopped her.

His kisses were soft and tantalising, draining her of
the will to resist. A shiver of delight ran through her
as he began to plant a trail of kisses, finding all the
most sensitive areas—throat and eyelids and the
corners of her lips. He was still holding her to him
with one arm, for her feet did not touch bottom, and
he seemed to know that she was in no state to tread
water. With the other hand he began an exploration of

her body, moulding the shape of her wet hips and waist beneath his fingers. Teri fought hard to remain detached, but it was a fast-losing battle. She had been kissed before, but never like this, so erotically, and never by such a man.

At this moment she did not remember that he had tricked her, that he did not even seem to like her very much. There were only the dictates of a fevered mind and a body that throbbed with a mixture of anguish and delight. Like a starving person craving bread, she craved for his kisses; she felt she could never get enough of them.

His hand moved upwards to her breasts, exploring them with a sensuousness that pushed her over the edge of control. With her feet holding on to one of his calves, she arched herself towards him, putting her arms around his neck and burying her hands in the thick wet hair.

'Kiss me!' It was a plea, and it came out without shame or conscious thought on her part.

Incredibly, Sloan loosened the arms that were around his neck and pushed her a little away from him. Dazed, she stared up at him, and saw that his own eyes were hooded.

'Sloan. . . .'

'The others must be wondering where we are. Any moment now and your greedy knight will be here looking for you.'

He didn't want to kiss her. She felt suddenly ill. All he had done was make a point, had shown her that if she wanted sexual enjoyment she could get it as easily from him as from Bruce. Sloan had shown her that he could arouse her—but he himself was not aroused at all.

Something of her feelings must have revealed themselves to him. Roughly he said, 'We both know what the next step had to be, and the ocean is not the place for it.'

That made sense, but Teri was in no mood for sense. All she knew was that he had rejected her. It was a rejection that hurt. 'Thank God for the ocean,' she managed in a tight voice.

'You don't mean that, and you know it. You were asking for more love, Teri, but there's a point beyond which a man can't go without losing control.'

'Give me my bikini!' she hissed through her teeth.

'We'll reach that point another time, Teri, in my bed or yours.'

'Never!' she exclaimed passionately. 'Are you going to give me that bikini, or do I go back to the beach without it?'

'To inflame the wretched Bruce to some genuine emotion?' His voice was harsh. 'Keep still, I'll put it on for you.'

'I can manage.'

'That would be some feat. You still can't touch bottom,' he reminded her dryly.

And that was true, humiliating though it was to acknowledge the fact. Supporting herself with her feet on his legs, Teri kept her face averted as Sloan slipped the bikini over her shoulders and fastened the clasp at her back. She tried to ignore the excitement she felt, even now, when she knew that Sloan had had his motives for arousing her. 'I'm crazy,' she thought, 'quite crazy. And I didn't know it was in me to feel this way.'

'Honey!' Bruce came to meet her as she made her way out of the water. 'You were out there a long time.'

'Not all that long,' she defended herself lightly, disliking the note of accusation she detected in his tone.

'Bruce was getting jealous.' Virginia's smile was somewhat malicious. 'He noticed two heads bobbing about close together on the water. I think he imagined Sloan making love to you.'

'If he was worried, he should have investigated.' Teri's tone was still light. She was learning their language, but she didn't enjoy using it.

'Bruce doesn't like cold water.' said Virginia, and Miranda put in on a brittle laugh, 'Sloan doesn't make love in the ocean—he prefers the comfort of a warm bed!'

Spoken with the complacent smugness of one who knew. Pain throbbed in Teri's temples, and she was swept with a sudden wave of nausea. She turned abruptly, shutting from her vision three faces that studied her with expressions that varied from malice to smiling calculation. She saw Jill, engrossed in her sand-castle, and she also saw Sloan, swimming the waves now with long easy strokes.

Turning back, she said to Bruce, 'I think I'll go.'

'The day's just begun,' he protested.

'I'm a little tired. And Jill could do with a nap.'

'She's having the time of her life.'

Which was true. Teri felt guilty at depriving the little girl of an extra hour or two on the beach, but she herself could take just so much. There would be other sunny days on the beach. She would bring Jill again, but alone.

'I'd like to go all the same,' she persisted with a calmness that hid her pain. 'May I take your car, Bruce? You could go back with the others.'

His face was just the slightest bit sullen as he assented. 'Oh, all right, then. But I won't let you cut short our future dates, Teri honey.'

Teri got back to Vins Doux to find Emma concluding a conversation with Esther, the housekeeper, a look of frustration on her normally placid face. A problem in the kitchen perhaps, Teri surmised, though without too much interest—her own problems were sufficiently overwhelming just then.

'You're back early, dear,' Emma remarked as Esther, looking worried herself, walked away.

'I'd had enough sun, and Jill can do with a nap. I've found a wonderful book, Emma, I think I'll do some reading.'

'As long as you keep an eye on Jill at the same time. Jessie's not around to help with her today.'

'That's all right. It's Sunday and I didn't expect any help.'

'I don't even know where she is. Neither does Esther.' The look of frustration was back.

'Something's wrong?' Teri asked in quick concern.

'It could be nothing, of course. On the other hand. . . .' Emma hesitated a moment. 'Teri dear, I know Jessie talks to you sometimes. Does the name Lucas mean anything to you?'

'Lucas? No. . . . Should it?'

'By rights it should not,' Emma said grimly. 'Lucas is a young man who has spent some time behind prison bars.'

'Why?'

'For stealing a car.'

'And he's Jessie's boy-friend?' Teri asked intuitively.

'He was. I think she fancied herself in love with him at one time.' Emma took a breath. 'He was released recently.'

'Do you think Jessie is with him?'

'I've forbidden her to see him.'

Forbidden? A strong word to apply to a girl in love. A word Teri had not thought would be used by the kindly, easy-going Emma—who at this moment looked anything but easy-going.

'For her own good,' Emma added. 'That young man would give her nothing but grief.'

'Jessie may have gone out somewhere on her own,' Teri suggested lightly.

'Maybe.' But Emma did not look convinced.

As she herself was not convinced, Teri thought a little later. Having settled Jill for her nap, she had taken her book out into the garden. But her mind was not on the history of wine-making. It was on the sweet-faced housemaid who had endeared herself to Teri with her kindness to Jill. It came to Teri that Jessie had not been quite herself yesterday. Her manner had been more reserved than usual, her eyes over-bright.

I should have asked her if something was wrong, Teri thought, on a pang of regret. Perhaps if I hadn't been so wrapped up in my own problems I'd have done so.

Her heart went out to the girl who was in love with a man who was inaccessible. We have something in common, she thought. The man I love is inaccessible too.

Her breath jerked. For the first time she had admitted to herself that she was in love with Sloan. Was it true? Surely not! Oh God, please don't let me love Sloan. Please! I don't *want* to love him. There's no future for me if I do.

Forcing her eyes back to the pages in front of her, she tried to read. But she did not see the words. What she saw was the ocean, and the laughing eyes of a tanned and handsome pirate as he held an emerald bikini out of her reach. And what she felt was not the hot sun on her face but the texture of a rough chest against her bare damp breasts.

Oh God! she whispered again, more despairingly this time. Closing the book and tucking it under her arm, she began to walk. A wind had risen, and it stung her cheeks and blew her hair backwards from her face, and she rejoiced in the feel of it. Perhaps, miraculously, it could blow this unwanted craziness from her mind and her heart.

CHAPTER NINE

LIFE at Vins Doux began to settle into a routine. Virginia took leave from her modelling job and started to organise a day-care centre for the farm-workers. In her aunt's presence her eagerness was boundless. 'All those darling children,' she exclaimed. 'I have such plans for them!'

'You'll go on taking an interest in the project after you go back to Cape Town?'

'Try and stop me! I've never worked with children before, Aunt Emma, I didn't know what fun it could be. Oh yes, I'll be here regularly and see that things go the way they should.'

'I'm so glad, Virginia, I really am.' Emma was moved.

Later in the day Teri spent some time with Jill in the garden. While the little girl played with the rubber doll, still her favourite toy, Teri relaxed in the shade of a gnarled and ancient oak tree. She was half asleep when she heard Virginia talking, her voice carrying across the still air.

'It's just the limit, Bruce!'

'True. But I suppose you've no option but to make the best of it.'

'As you're doing, brother dear!'

'I'm beginning to like the wine business.'

'And the girl that goes with it. Hell, Bruce, I don't give a damn what you do—but this day-care really is the bloody limit! If the girls at the agency could see me pandering to a bunch of snotty-nosed toddlers they'd die laughing!'

'I doubt you pander to them,' Bruce laughed. They changed direction as they walked further and with the wind now behind them the rest of their words were lost.

Teri was not sorry. She had an aversion to eavesdropping. Not that she had learned something new. She had suspected that Virginia's sweetness was a way of covering her true feelings. And that was sad, for it seemed to mean a great deal to Emma that her relatives should take an interest in the bequest that was to be theirs.

For his part, Bruce really did seem to be interested. He talked enthusiastically of all he was learning, and the enthusiasm did not seem in the least feigned. Teri chided herself for thinking, even for one moment, that it might be. Suspicion was a dreadful thing, she decided, and wished Sloan had not implanted it in her mind. Bruce continued to show her affection, there were even times when he intimated that he had more than mere friendship on his mind. Though Teri did not rise to such overtures, she could not help wondering about them. Quite likely her appeal for Bruce was in fact enhanced because of the benefits that he supposed would accompany her. That did not mean that his affection was feigned, just as there was no reason to suppose that his interest in Vins Doux was anything but genuine.

Teri spent most of her days in the library. The pile of notes grew as her research took shape. There were so many wonderful books in the wood-panelled room at Vins Doux. She read not only about wine-making, but about the history of the Cape, about the men and women who had made that history. For a librarian who loved to explore the past, the days she spent researching were idyllic.

Almost idyllic. Absorbed in a book, she would

suddenly find herself thinking of Sloan. He seemed to come to mind with amazing ease. She had only to read of some strong-minded historical figure, and Sloan's face would fill the page. She tried hard to stop thinking about him. Sometimes she was successful, more often not.

There were days when she hardly saw him. It was not often that he joined the others for meals. Teri wondered where he ate, where he lived. He did not live in the main house, that much she knew. On that first evening at Vins Doux, Emma had referred to his quarters. Teri would have given much to know where they were—sheer curiosity, nothing more, she told herself—but in her wanderings around the estate she never saw them. Emma would have been able to tell her, but Teri did not want to ask—Emma was already too conscious of the tense relationship between Sloan and herself, and the girl had the uneasy feeling that she was amused by it.

There were other people she could have asked. Jessie or Esther. Even Virginia and Bruce would have been able to answer the question. But Teri found herself oddly reluctant to bring up Sloan's name. She did not know if she could trust herself to do so casually. There was also the knowledge that she did not want to discuss him with others.

She was not so naïve that she did not know how she felt about him. She loved him. She had fallen in love with the tall rugged-faced man. There was a time when she had tried to tell herself that she was merely affected by his dynamic looks; that his sole appeal was sexual and physical. Now she knew that she had been fooling herself. She loved him, probably she would always love him. And all she would get in return was a broken heart.

If I was sensible I'd leave Vins Doux tomorrow, she

told herself when the words on the page before her took on their customary blur. I'd put as much distance as possible between Sloan and myself and make quite sure that I never set eyes on him again. I might meet another man, learn to love him instead.

And that would take a miracle, Teri knew. She had been in Sloan's arms, had been kissed by him. It would be impossible to feel stirred by anyone else. A miracle? It would take more than that.

Besides, there was no way she *could* leave Vins Doux. She had given her word to Emma. There was also Jill to consider. Every day the little girl's cheeks had more colour. The small body was filling out, and the cough had virtually disappeared. Teri wished that Louise could see her—her friend would be amazed at the transformation.

'Sloan coming for supper tonight?' Virginia asked one day at lunch.

'Not that I know of,' said her aunt.

'Mind if I ask him?'

Without waiting for an answer the girl went to the phone. The conversation was short, and when Virginia rejoined the others she looked disgruntled. 'He's going out. What does he see in Miranda, I wonder?'

'She's very attractive.' There was a slight edge to Bruce's voice, but Teri did not question it. The fact that Sloan was dating Miranda was not news. There was not a night when she did not torture herself with visions of them together. When she did not see them talking, laughing, making love. . . . Nevertheless, when the fact was put into words she felt a pain that was almost physical.

'What do you think of her, Teri?' Virginia asked.

It was hard to speak over the dryness of her throat. 'I agree with Bruce,' Teri managed. 'She's attractive '

'Fancy her chances with Sloan? My God, Teri, you look awful. Don't say you like him too!'

'Of course not,' Teri managed lightly. 'Just feeling a bit under the weather. If you'll excuse me, I still want to get some reading done this afternoon.'

She saw their faces as she rose from her chair. Virginia's momentary curiosity had left her—her interest in others never lasted long—and the restlessness was back. Bruce was oddly tight-lipped. Emma, who had remained silent during the brief interchange, was regarding her thoughtfully.

Teri spent the remainder of the day in the library, as well as most of the next morning. For once the books held no appeal for her. Visions of Sloan and Miranda had made for fitful sleep, and now her head ached. When Bruce asked her to go out for lunch with him she agreed, not out of a desire to spend time with him, but because she thought the outing would be a welcome diversion from thoughts she seemed unable to shut out.

A scenic ocean drive led to the restaurant which was set among silver trees and purple proteas on a sunny mountain slope. The exterior was cheerful and inviting, and as Teri got out of the car her spirits lifted. A change of scene had been even more necessary than she had realised.

'This is lovely.' She turned a smiling face to Bruce as they followed the waitress in. 'It's so. . . .'

The words died on her lips. Sloan was at a table, and Miranda was with him.

Had Teri been alone she would have walked out of the restaurant before they looked up and saw her. As it was, Bruce had his hand on her waist, and it seemed to her fevered mind as if he was actually pushing her forward.

Miranda was talking, and Sloan was listening to her

attentively. With any luck Teri could pass them without being noticed. The hand was still at her back—friendly yet firm—when they reached the fateful table.

'I always knew we'd work things out,' Teri heard Miranda say, and then, on a new note, 'Why, look who's here!'

Sloan lifted his head. His eyes moved from Teri to Bruce, then back again. Blue eyes that were devoid of any expression. Only the hardness of his mouth indicated his displeasure.

Miranda and Bruce said hello more or less simultaneously, and Sloan murmured a curt greeting of his own, but Teri, to her shame, found that her mouth was so dry that she was unable to say anything at all.

'Enjoy your meal,' Bruce said pleasantly. 'I see our table is ready.'

Teri walked blindly further. A waitress came to take the order, and Teri indicated to Bruce that he should decide for them both. It made no difference what he chose; she knew she would not taste the food, however delicious it might be. She didn't even know if she could eat.

Unwillingly her eyes were drawn to Sloan and Miranda. 'You knew they'd be here, didn't you?' she asked in a low voice, the first words she had uttered since entering the restaurant.

'Anything's possible—always.'

An uncorked bottle of wine rested in an ice-bucket beside Sloan. As Teri watched, Miranda raised her glass and Sloan's came up to meet it. Over the soft sound of clinking glass came the murmur of laughing voices, the words indistinguishable.

Teri's throat felt raw. Fiercely she blinked back the tears that had gathered behind her eyelids. She would *not* cry.

'Why did you bring me here?' she asked, when she could speak again.

Bruce smiled. 'To eat, obviously, my darling girl.'

Disregarding the endearment, she forced herself to meet his eyes. 'I think you had another reason.'

Eyes that had always been warm until now grew suddenly cold. 'Okay, so I thought it might be a good idea if you saw where Sloan's affections lie.'

'I knew already. Why should I care anyway?'

'I've seen the way you look at him.' There was an unexpected edge of cruelty in Bruce's tone. 'Sloan isn't for you, Teri.'

'A warning?'

'A friendly one.'

A brutal one. More brutal than Sloan's had been when he'd warned her to stay away from Bruce.

Somehow she forced herself to smile. 'I don't need warnings. I can take care of myself.'

After a moment Bruce said, 'You've proved that, haven't you? Do you keep in touch with Jill's father?'

There was something blatant and rather insolent in his expression. It was as unexpected as the cruelty in his tone had been.

Teri felt a chill run through her. 'I think,' she said, with all the dignity at her disposal, 'that we should change the subject.'

'Fine with me. Sloan and Miranda seem to be celebrating something rather special. Do you think you and I could have a celebration of our own, Teri?'

She stared at him dazed, wondering if she had understood him correctly. 'We've nothing to celebrate,' she protested uncertainly.

'We could have.' He reached over and took her hand. 'You must know how I feel about you, Teri. Will you marry me?'

This is a dream, Teri thought. And then she felt

Bruce's hand tighten on hers. He was smiling as he waited for her to answer, and she knew it wasn't a dream.

'We hardly know each other,' she murmured at length.

'We'll have time for that.'

Teri felt rather than saw the sudden silence at Sloan's table. Darting a deliberately playful look at Bruce, she said, 'Would you still want me if I were not in line for a share of Vins Doux?'

It was a provocative question, an appallingly provocative question. The smile froze on Bruce's face, and his fingers bit cruelly into the delicate wrist.

And then the smile widened once more. 'Sweetheart, I didn't know you were a tease.'

She could have repeated the question, could have insisted on an answer, but none was necessary.

'*Will* you marry me?'

'I have no plans to marry anyone,' she told him quite truthfully. 'Not now. Perhaps never.'

Neither did she plan to look at Sloan. Treacherously, of their own accord, her eyes moved his way. Incredibly he looked up at that moment and his eyes met hers. Two pairs of eyes locked together for what seemed an interminable time. Teri felt her heart pounding like a mad thing against her ribs. Then Sloan turned back to Miranda, and slowly, very slowly Teri's heartbeat returned to normal.

Sloan came to supper two nights later. Despite the fact that Teri had steeled herself to be calm and relaxed, her senses clamoured at sight of him.

Only Emma was missing from the little group that had gathered in the sun-room for a before-dinner drink. Sloan sat back in a cane chair, one long leg resting casually across the other. In beige slacks and a darker shirt open at the throat, he looked so attractive that Teri felt her pulses beat faster. Casually he sipped a beer, and laughed as Virginia touched his cheek in a flirtatious caress, and Teri wondered how Miranda would feel were she present to see it.

'Wonder what's keeping Aunt Emma?' Bruce mused.

'I don't mind waiting.' Virginia dimpled a seductive smile at Sloan. 'I hear you and Miranda have been celebrating.'

Sloan did not look discomfited. 'Bruce tells tales?'

'When he knows his sister is interested. Want to tell us about it?'

Teri's breath caught in her throat. Sloan looked across at her, almost as if he had detected the tiny hiss of sound, then back at Virginia. 'In good time,' he grinned, looking disgustingly smug.

Where was Emma? Teri could not stand the tension a moment longer. It would be a relief to go through to the dining-room, even though she would not enjoy the meal. She could not remember the last meal she had enjoyed.

Just then the door opened and Emma came into the room. Her eyes were bright and her cheeks flamed with colour, and Teri saw at once that she was angry.

'Sorry I'm late. I was delayed by some news.'

'Bad news?' Teri asked concerned.

'Bad—but not unexpected. Jessie is pregnant.'

Sloan said, 'Lucas?'

'Who else? I'd forbidden her to see him. My God, the girl has no sense! He stole a car, he's been in jail, I warned her that he would give her nothing but grief.'

'She should have listened to you,' Virginia said sympathetically. 'Now I suppose she wants your help.'

'She hasn't quite asked for it in so many words. I'm

so furious, if I do decide to help it will have to be on my terms.'

'I think that's terrible.' Teri's words were clear and distinct in the silent room.

'I beg your pardon!' Emma looked at her incredulously.

'If anybody but Lucas were the father you wouldn't be so angry.'

'That's true. . . .' Emma conceded.

'You forbade Jessie to see him, and she went ahead nevertheless, and now you're angry.'

'Why do I get the feeling,' Emma Roland asked ominously, 'that you're criticising me?'

It was very quiet in the dining-room. Virginia looked shocked. Bruce looked stunned. He shook his head slightly, he was throwing a silent warning, one Teri decided to ignore.

Sloan's expression was difficult to read. Teri was not in the mood to analyse it.

She took a breath. 'I don't mean to offend you, Emma, but it's Jessie's life. I don't believe you have the right to tell her how to lead it.'

'Well, really, Teri!' This from Virginia. 'You're asking Aunt Emma to condone what Jessie's done, and to help her into the bargain!'

'I'm just saying that she has no right to condemn Jessie,' Teri said stubbornly.

'I will not have my rights questioned, Teri.' Emma spoke very quietly. 'Not by you, not by anyone.'

'And I,' Teri said just as quietly, 'will do everything I can to help Jessie.'

'You don't know what you're saying, Teri—after all, Aunt Emma has done everything for. . . .' The flow of Bruce's words stopped abruptly as the door opened and Esther called Emma to the telephone.

When the door had closed Bruce was the first to speak. 'Cool it, Teri.'

She looked at him frigidly. 'You're thinking of my share in Vins Doux?'

After the slightest of moments Bruce said, 'Yes.'

Now was not the moment to disclose that she had declined her share. Her promise to Emma still stood. But after she had left Vins Doux—Emma would not want her here after this—the others would learn the truth.

She said, 'I stand by everything I said.'

'You can't mean that.'

'I do. If Jessie loves Lucas—and I believe she does—then what she does is her own business.'

'I can see why Teri would support Jessie,' Virginia drawled. 'She was in the same position herself once. I'm not surprised, are you, Sloan?'

Tensing, Teri curled her nails into her palms and looked at Sloan. Thus far there had been no word out of him. There had been only the expression she had not tried to analyse. An expression, she realised now, that had been akin to surprise, as if he had come face to face with something he did not expect. The expression had been momentary. It was gone now. The blue eyes were hooded, impossible to read.

So you condemn me too, Sloan? Teri thought. Lifting her chin, she said aloud, 'I *do* understand Jessie.' The words had the sound of a challenge.

'Where is Jill's father?' Virginia asked conversationally.

Teri answered her flatly. 'He's dead.'

Leave it at that. Please, just leave it at that. You don't know the wounds that are being re-opened.

But Bruce said, 'I asked you if you still had contact with him. You didn't say he was dead.'

She remembered the question. It had been put to her in the restaurant, while just yards away Sloan and

Miranda had been celebrating. 'I told you then that I wanted to change the subject.'

Bruce looked uncertain a moment. There was nothing more he could say, surely. Yet, 'You loved him?' he asked.

This can't be happening to me! I have to be dreaming.

On a wave of pain, Teri closed her eyes. She could see her parents, her mother and father playing with the baby whom they had adored.

Opening her eyes, she looked around her. For a few moments she had felt as if she was elsewhere, back in the rambling house that had once been home. It was almost a shock to see three faces staring at her. Bruce and Virginia, openly curious. Sloan, more grim than she had ever seen him.

'I loved Jill's father,' she said quietly, feeling as if she would choke. Virginia seemed about to say something but Teri put up a hand to silence her. 'Don't ask me any more.'

Blindly she wheeled and left the room.

Later that evening Teri opened her door to a knock. 'May I come in?' Emma asked.

'Yes, of course.'

The older woman walked to the window and stared a few seconds into the night. Then she turned.

'I'm sorry,' she said.

'Sorry?' Teri's voice was unsteady.

'I may be a foolish woman, Teri, but I'm not that foolish. You stood up for what you believed in, and you were right.'

'Emma. . . .'

'Let me finish. You *were* right, my dear. I was wrong to think I could tell Jessie how to live her life.'

'I believe she loves Lucas,' Teri said gently.

'She does. I've also learned that Lucas deeply

regrets the fact he ever got into bad company. His friends dared him to steal the car and he was too weak to say no. He paid dearly for the weakness.'

'Will Jessie marry him?' Teri asked.

'Yes. And I intend to help them, God knows I can afford it.'

'Oh, Emma, I'm so glad!'

For the first time Emma Roland smiled. 'You don't know how glad *I* am—for coming to my senses in time.'

'I have to apologise too,' said Teri. 'I was very rude to you.'

'You were honest. And that's more than I can say for my family. Neither Virginia nor Bruce are angels in their private lives, I do know that, yet they were prepared to side with me, ready to condemn Jessie because they thought it was what I wanted to hear.'

'You don't know that.'

'Yes, Teri, I do. For too many years I've been surrounded by people who pay me lip service because I'm a rich woman. Until I met you I thought Sloan was the only exception.'

Sloan. Always Sloan.

'You befriended me when you had no idea who I was. Today you showed your honesty and fearlessness.'

'If you say any more I'll get conceited,' Teri smiled over the lump in her throat.

'I will say one more thing,' Emma added. 'You can forget about leaving Vins Doux.'

Teri stared at the older woman. 'How did you know?'

'I know you, my dear, and you have a face that is transparent.'

Do you also know that I love Sloan? That I can't bear the thought of him getting married to Miranda? That leaving Vins Doux would mean that I need never see them together, as man and wife, as lovers?

'You gave me a promise,' reminded Emma.

'I know.'

'I don't intend to release you from it.'

'You're a ruthless woman, Emma,' sighed Teri.

'A tigress,' her friend countered cheerfully. 'Sleep well, my dear. Tomorrow we'll talk of ways to help Jessie.'

Teri finished breakfast early next morning, before the others had even made their appearance. She lingered over her coffee a while, musing over the happenings of last night. She was glad she had made her peace with Emma. The time would come when she would have to leave Vins Doux, but she had grown very fond of Emma Roland, and it was a relief that the eventual parting would be friendly rather than hostile.

She finished her coffee and was about to leave the room when her eye was caught by a stool in one corner, a replica of one she had seen in a book just yesterday. Filled with sudden excitement, she went to it.

Kneeling, she began to examine the lovely hand-carved wood. At the sound of footsteps she did not turn, and even when two trouser-clad legs stopped beside her she did not look up.

'Bruce, this stool must be two hundred years old!' Her voice bubbled with enthusiasm. 'Isn't it gorgeous! Heavens, but it must be worth a fortune!'

There was no answer from above. That could only mean that Bruce was no connoisseur of fine furniture. Unconcerned, Teri continued to study the carving. Only gradually did she feel a prickling of the hairs on her neck, and her body tensed.

Very slowly she looked up. Sloan was looking down at her, and his eyes were anything but amused.

'It's a lovely piece,' she said uncertainly, wondering why he looked quite so angry.

'And worth a fortune, as you guessed. Hoping the stool will form a part of your share?'

The words as much as the hardness in his tone brought her to her feet. 'You're in a fine temper this morning.'

'Let me make the accusations.'

She loved him. She also had to concede that he was impossibly arrogant. 'What else do you think I'm after? Have you checked the silver lately? I could be stowing it away, making sure I get more than my share.'

He made an irritable gesture. 'Don't be flippant. I came here to talk to you.'

If only her heart would stop its stupid leaping. This was no time to be thinking how dynamic he looked. 'We've nothing to talk about.'

'We have.'

'My greed?' Teri asked sarcastically.

Blue eyes were hooded. 'We'll leave that subject for now. It's Bruce I want to discuss. The pair of you.'

'Do you think of us as a pair?'

'You certainly looked the part in the restaurant.'

And how do you think *you* looked, you and Miranda? Toasting each other with wine, or was it champagne? Happy that things had worked out as you'd always wanted.

'I don't want to talk about it.'

'I do. In fact I came here last night for that reason. And a fine mess it turned out to be. Teri, I've given you one warning already.'

'I don't have to heed your warnings, Sloan.'

His lips thinned. 'You've been seeing a lot of each other?'

He had no right to put her on the spot, she thought,

and decided to lie. 'A fair amount. That worries you, Sloan?'

Something flickered in his eyes. Then he said harshly, 'Only because you and Bruce may well destroy Vins Doux.'

'You think the worst of us, then?' It was amazing that she could sustain the conversation with such calm.

'I see the pair of you as fortune-hunters.'

Her calmness deserted her as anger flamed inside her. 'How dare you, Sloan! Are you any better? An employee of Vins Doux who will now have a quarter of the estate to call your own. Who are you to judge us?'

As she saw her own anger mirrored in Sloan's eyes, Teri became taut. She had provoked him, and Sloan, she knew, could be dangerous when provoked. A small shiver of fear ran down her spine; at the same time she was also conscious of excitement.

His jaw had tightened, and the eyes that raked her face held an ominous glint. What would he say? Do?

It was a moment or two before he spoke, and when he did his tone was unexpectedly mild. 'I think, Teri, that you and I should spend the day together.'

Her senses leaped. Almost, she said yes—despite Miranda. Despite the cold contempt that was in Sloan's eyes whenever he looked at her; it was there now.

Sanity came to her aid just in time. 'You're crazy!'

A hand reached out, closing over her wrist, the fingers like burning steel on the delicate skin. 'You like to goad me, don't you?'

'All I did was refuse an invitation,' she said hardily, and wondered if he could feel the racing pulse.

'An invitation?' Neither of them had heard Virginia come into the room. 'Sounds exciting. What kind of invitation?'

The grip on Teri's wrist was abruptly released as Sloan muttered, 'I asked Teri to spend the day with me. She refused.'

'Well now!' Virginia was watching them both, openly curious. 'If our little child-mother lets the invitation go begging I'll be happy to take it up instead.'

She was smiling, the green eyes slanting and catlike. A little like Bruce's, Teri thought, and wondered why she had not noticed the similarity before. There was malice in the smile. To Teri, her emotions already raw, the malicious words and smile were a goad. Throwing Sloan a smile of her own, she said, 'I've changed my mind, I'd love to spend the day with you.'

'Can you be ready in half an hour?'

'Of course.'

Ready for what? Where were they going? And what should she wear? Questions that might have been answered if Sloan had told her what he intended.

Jessie, a radiant Jessie today, took Jill down to the kitchen for her breakfast. Perplexed, Teri stood before her wardrobe, and wondered why any encounter with Sloan always made her uncertain what to wear. The primrose sundress with the narrow shoulder-straps and pleated skirt was probably unsuitable. She decided to wear it nevertheless.

In the sun-room she found Emma talking to Sloan. 'I shouldn't be leaving Jill like this,' said Teri.

'I'll be with her, and Jessie is her devoted shadow.'

'Running out of excuses?' Sloan's eyes held a glimmer of wicked amusement. He studied her lazily, but she knew he missed no detail of her appearance— the dress which showed her slenderly curved figure to its best advantage, the bare legs in the dainty sandals; the newly-washed hair which she had loosened from its snood and which now hung soft and shining around her face.

Teri wished she could stop the colour from surging to her cheeks. 'I wasn't making an excuse.'

'Of course you weren't,' said Emma, smiling as she walked with them to the door.

CHAPTER TEN

OUTSIDE the house a car was waiting, the sleek silver vehicle which brought memory flooding back each time Teri saw it. As Sloan started the car along the oak-lined avenue of Vins Doux, Teri was aware of a familiar ripple of awareness. He still had not told her where they were going, and she had not asked. Her eyes were turned to the window, but all she saw was Sloan. He was in her eyes, in her mind, in her heart. She did not need to look at him, for he was clear in every part of her being. As he always would be. Long after she had left Vins Doux. Perhaps for ever.

They came to the main road, and to her surprise Sloan did not turn in the direction of Cape Town, the only direction which she knew thus far. He took the opposite turn instead. They had not gone far when he turned again, on to a road not unlike the one that led to Vins Doux. And now Teri could no longer contain her curiosity.

'We're going to visit someone?'

The face that turned to her was amused. 'Wait and see.'

The road widened at the approach to a pair of white gates set in a stone wall. Over the gates, in wrought iron letters, was the name 'Bienvenue'.

'The name rings a bell.' Teri's brow wrinkled. 'Oh, I have it. The wine we had that first evening ... Emma's favourite. It was bottled here?'

'Right.'

'It's a lovely name. Bienvenue—welcome.'

'Which you are,' said Sloan.

Teri did not know why her breathing quickened a little as they passed through the gates and started down another long avenue. Anticipation stirred along her spine together with a slight feeling of dread. She knew suddenly that Sloan had brought her here for a very particular reason.

Bienvenue was indeed a wine estate. Teri soon realised that it was even vaster than Vins Doux, even more impressive, though she would not have believed such a thing could be possible. It was as if the vines here had an extra bloom, as if the bunches of grapes were even more lushly inviting.

Her breath jerked in her throat as they rounded a bend and a house came suddenly into sight. At the same moment the car slowed.

'Well?' There was an odd note in Sloan's voice.

'It's fantastic!'

Dimly she remembered reacting this way when she had seen Vins Doux the first time. Nearly she said, 'It's even more beautiful than Vins Doux,' but she stopped herself in time, for the words would have been in some way disloyal.

And yet the house *was* in some way even more beautiful. Like Vins Doux, its architecture was Cape Dutch. The curved gables were there, the white walls and the wooden windows. But it seemed to have an extra graciousness, an extra spendour.

'Who lives here?' Teri wanted to ask as Sloan started the car once more and drove further. One look at his face changed her mind. She could see only his profile, but she sensed a tautness that had not been there before, and she kept silent. In good time she would discover why he had brought her here.

A neatly-dressed woman—the housekeeper, Teri guessed—was watering a gardenia in a big earthenware trough at the foot of the steps. She looked up as the car drew up, and when they had got out, she said, 'Two phone calls while you were out, Mr Sloan.'

Teri felt the colour drain from her cheeks. It took every ounce of strength she possessed to control her features as the man at her side said, 'You can tell me about them later. Teri, I want you to meet Letitia. Letitia, this is Miss Malloy.'

Letitia acknowledged the introduction politely, but her eyes held a veiled look of curiosity. 'The tea is ready. Shall I bring it to the rose-garden?' she asked.

'Thank you.' Sloan put a hand under Teri's elbow as the housekeeper walked away. 'Tea first, it seems. You can see the house later.'

Teri maintained her numb composure until she was sure they were out of earshot, and then she turned on him. 'Why didn't you tell me?'

He shrugged. 'You never asked.'

'You let me think you lived at Vins Doux.'

'I don't recall ever having said so.'

It was hard to think when the fingers on her elbow moved slightly to caress the silken skin of her inner arm. 'I believed you had quarters somewhere on the property. And Emma never told me. . . .'

She bit her lip and fell silent. There were things Emma had never told Sloan either. She had kept a secret for Teri. What was it she had said? 'I'm good at keeping secrets. . . .' And there had been laughter in her eyes.

The rose-garden was a little way from the house. The roses were in bloom, a glorious profusion of reds and yellows and whites. Sloan stopped and lightly touched the petals of a salmon-coloured bloom. 'One of my newest.'

An unusual rose, and very beautiful, but Teri's mind was on other things. 'Sloan.' She took a breath before plunging into the question to which she sensed the answer—and hoped she was wrong. 'Are you employed at Bienvenue too?'

There was a hint of humour in the eyes that met hers. 'No.'

'You can't mean. . . . You don't *own* Bienvenue?'

'As a matter of fact I do.' A hand lifted to her cheek, curving around it. 'Do you mind?'

The sensuousness of the touch made her tremble. Teri forced herself to stand very still. 'Why should I mind?' she asked lightly.

Why indeed? What with Miranda, and his dislike of Teri herself, until this moment Sloan had seemed inaccessible enough. This latest turn of events had removed him so far from her orbit that he might as well have his home on another planet.

Letitia arrived with the tea-tray, and Teri was glad of the distraction. 'Why don't you do the honours?' Sloan suggested.

The tea-set was silver, antique and beautifully wrought, and the cups were of a porcelain so delicate that Teri thought a careless flick of a finger might break them. She was glad she had left Jill at Vins Doux.

'Do you know,' Sloan remarked softly, 'you look just right pouring that tea.'

'Nothing to it.' Teri's smile hid the ache in her heart. She *felt* right, pouring the tea, handing Sloan his cup. Felt that she could happily perform the same task over and over again through the years. She was not so naïve that she did not understand the picture that had come, almost of itself, into her mind. And she was intelligent enough to know that the sooner she pushed it from her, the better. Today was a once-only event, a cameo that she would keep in her memory. It was Miranda who would pour the tea on all those other days that stretched into the future. Miranda who would share Sloan's thoughts and dreams. Who would lie in one bed with him and glory in his love-making. . . .

Teri gave an involuntary shake of the head as she thrust the thought from her. A thought that was too painful to endure.

'That *was* emphatic,' she heard the bubble of laughter in Sloan's throat. 'Care to share the joke?'

'It wasn't a joke.' Her voice was low. So close was she to tears at this moment that any pretence of casualness was beyond her.

'Teri?'

'Why did you bring me here?'

His eyes grew serious. 'You seemed to think I had no right to warn you about Bruce. You implied that I too was just out to get what I could.'

'I didn't know. . . .'

'How could you?'

Virginia or Bruce could have mentioned Sloan's status, but perhaps they had assumed that she knew it. Emma could have enlightened her—but Emma, it seemed, had had her reasons for keeping silent.

She looked around her. The rose-garden was on a high piece of ground. Sloping away from it on three sides were the vineyards, a vista of shimmering purple and gold beneath the midday sun.

'Why do you want a share of Vins Doux?' She made a gesture. 'You have so much land of your own.' She looked at him, wondering if she had transgressed the bounds of politeness, yet needing an answer all the same. 'You can't need any more?'

'I don't need it. Bienvenue is not the only property I own, Teri. I never wanted even a part of Vins Doux.'

'Then why?'

'Have you ever seen,' he asked slowly, 'what

happens to a place when the wrong people gain control? People who don't know what it is to work. Who are only interested in quick profits, and who put back nothing in return? The most valuable estates can be ruined in the time it takes to buy a fancy yacht and a few expensive cars.'

'You think that's what would happen to Vins Doux with Bruce and Virginia in control. And with me, of course.' The last words were an afterthought, quickly added, for Sloan could not know that she had decided not to accept her share of the vineyards—unless Emma had talked, which seemed unlikely.

'Exactly.' His lips were set in a grim line. 'I've been looking after Vins Doux since Jonathan Roland died.'

'That's why Emma has given you a share?'

'Right again. I don't need it, Teri, but the place means a great deal to me. Almost as much as Bienvenue. I accepted because it's the only way I can ensure that Vins Doux will not be ruined by ignorance and greed.'

A little lifelessly, Teri said, 'I see now why you brought me here today.'

'There was another reason.' The inflection in his tone drew her eyes to him. 'I wanted you to see my home.'

He was searching her face, the small sun-kissed nose and cheeks the lips that had opened willingly beneath his, and in his eyes was an expression that sent a surge of adrenalin pumping through Teri's system.

She was all at once breathless. 'I'd like very much to see it.'

Tea finished, they made their way to the house. Miranda's future home. I'm crazy to allow Sloan to show it to me, Teri thought as she walked beside him up the steps that led to a solid oak door. I'll be more miserable afterwards. I should tell him to take me back to Vins Doux now, before I go any further. Her step slowed, almost halted.

'Teri?' Sloan was looking down at her. He was smiling, but in his eyes was something taut. His hand went to her waist, as if to urge her forwards. The tautness was in his hand too, Teri could feel it. And suddenly she herself felt taut. Without a word she walked on.

From a gracious entrance hall, wood-panelled and with a glorious Persian carpet in shades of green and white and peacock-blue, Sloan led her to the lounge, the dining-room, the library. All the rooms were beautiful, as Teri had known they would be. As with the exterior, there was a similarity with Vins Doux, for the houses had been built around the same time. There were the polished oak floors and the furnishings were mostly antique. But there were differences too. The feeling that Bienvenue was a special place was reinforced. It was impossible for Teri to see everything. The best she could do was absorb the impression of tradition and elegance. On another visit she could take in details.

The thought caught her up short. Would there be another visit? Unlikely. Sloan had brought her here today for a purpose. He had no reason to bring her again.

The knowledge did not make it easier to focus on specifics. The tautness that had come over Teri on the steps of the homestead was with her still. Added to it was an awareness of Sloan, of the sexuality and maleness that seemed to accompany him wherever he went. He was close beside her and the air between them seemed alive with electricity. It buzzed in Teri's ears, if she put out a hand it would shock her. Surely Sloan must feel it too. She glanced up at him. If he was aware of the vibrancy in the air between them his expression did not reveal it. The strong face was as aloof and stern as she had seen it and for a moment Teri wondered if she had offended him in some way.

Having seen the front part of the house, Teri was certain they would go back outside, back to Vins Doux. When Sloan took her into a corridor which could only lead to the bedroom wing, she looked up at him questioningly. The tautness she had glimpsed earlier had intensified, the hand on her wrist urged her on. All at once it was hard to breathe.

She lost count of the bedrooms. She was only aware of the tightness inside her, and of an aching hunger which she tried to suppress and could not.

It was with a feeling of inevitability that Teri watched Sloan open the last door. There was not even surprise as she went past him into a room that was all brown and gold. A room that was both elegant and masculine.

'Your bedroom?' It was a question that needed no answer, and she wished she had not asked it, for the words had come out too jerkily.

'Yes.'

She turned, intending to go past him, back to the door—and found him blocking it.

Her heart gave an uncomfortable leap in her chest. 'Sloan?'

He closed the door, softly but firmly. 'Teri.'

'It's a nice room.' Her voice was husky with betraying nervousness.

'I'm so glad you like it,' he said politely.

'Oh, I do. Shall we go on to the next room?'

'This is the last.'

'In that case I suppose it's time to go back to Vins Doux.'

He made no move away from the door. He looked very tall, very powerful, as he stood before it, coiled and alert as a jungle animal on a hunt. An unfortunate analogy at this particular moment, Teri thought, and her heartbeat became more painful.

Lifting her head and throwing him her most confident smile, she said, 'It really is time to go.'

'I think not.'

'You're playing with me, Sloan.'

'I'd like to play with you,' was the soft response.

A thrill of alarm ran through her as he took a step forward. The serpent, moving smoothly towards its victim. She took a quick step away, only to find the backs of her legs against the bed.

'Definitely the right direction.' Laughter bubbled in his throat, husky and seductive.

Putting up a hand—as if that could ward him off—she said, 'What do you want, Sloan?'

'You know what I want, my dearest.'

The endearment escaped her. She was only conscious of a longing that was greater than any she had ever experienced.

'It's what you want too,' he said, taking another step towards her.

Yes! I want you to kiss me, make love to me. God, how I want it!

Aloud she said, 'No! Let me go, Sloan.'

His eyes glittered. 'We have some unfinished business, you and I, Teri.'

She stared at him. 'Business?'

'A small matter of mud thrown at my car.'

'Oh, that.'

'That.'

'We could.... Couldn't we discuss it somewhere else?'

'I think this is the perfect place.' He was so close to her now that she could feel the heat of his body through the small space of air that separated them. A hand cupped her chin, the fingers burning where they touched her throat. She felt as if she was suffocating.

'Don't you agree?' he asked softly.

'Yes—I mean no! Sloan, you're confusing me!'

'Delightful!' The fingers moved, exploring the area beneath an ear, sending ripples of awareness down her spine. 'You always knew that one day there would be a settling.'

She had known it. Deep inside her she had known it. Had known too that it wuld not be simple. With Sloan, it seemed, nothing was ever simple.

'I could wash your car,' she suggested.

'I have a gardener who does that for me.' His breath was warm as it fanned down to cheeks that were already hot. 'I could give you a spanking, but I don't spank women.' His hands cupped her head, burying themselves in her hair. 'I could make love to you.'

'Sloan. . . .'

'Sloan, yes, make love to me—is that what you're saying?'

Yes!

'No, of course not. Sloan, I càn't!'

'Sloan, I can't,' he mimicked. With his hands still cupping her head he put her a little away from him, so that he could look into her eyes. 'You sound so innocent, Teri. Like a virgin.' His voice grew hard. 'The one thing you're not. You don't rebuff Bruce. And there's Jill's father. You've never wanted to discuss him.'

She closed her eyes. 'I still don't.'

She heard his small hissing intake of breath. Then he said, 'He's in the past anyway. This is what counts—the present. You and me, here, now. You put up a good pretence, Teri, but your body tells a different tale.'

His lips were teasing, tantalising. They spread a

trail across her face and throat, unerringly and erotically finding the most sensitive spots. With his tongue he traced the contours of her lips. By the time his mouth came down on hers she ached with longing. His kisses were passionate, demanding, evoking an answering response from her. Willingly she opened her mouth to his, exulting as he explored it.

His arms were around her now, holding her close, and she could feel the long hard length of him; hard thighs and calves straining against her own soft legs, hard-muscled chest in which the heart beat the same frenzied rhythm as her own.

This was how it had been in her dreams at night. This was how he had held her and kissed her. Except that the reality was more exciting than anything she had dreamed.

The drugging kisses, the hands that moved on her back, curving around to cup her breasts, drove the last remnants of sanity from her being. Mindlessly she pressed towards him, wrapping her arms around his neck.

'This is how you respond to Bruce?' Sloan asked once, when he lifted his head.

Later Teri would wonder why it was so important to thwart him. 'Of course,' she lied.

She heard him swear beneath his breath, and then he was kissing her again, more roughly this time. He might have been giving vent to some inexplicable anger, but after the first moment of outrage Teri did not think about that. His mouth on hers had become even fiercer, more demanding. His hands were doing things to her body that sent her senses whirling, so that she could not have protested had she wanted to. Overriding any rational thought was just a driving need for a fulfilment which only Sloan could provide.

She did not resist when she felt him pull down the

zip of her sun-dress or when he eased her bra over
her shoulders. She gave a little moan of pleasure when
his hands went to her breasts and began to cradle them
and caress the swelling nipples. And then her own
hands found the buttons of his shirt; she undid them
and let herself explore the muscled planes of his chest.

She heard him groan, and the sound filled her with
fierce joy. He wanted her as much as she wanted him.
There was something wonderful in that knowledge.

'Take the shirt off.' His tone was ragged, and she
heard his breathing quicken as she complied, slowly,
teasingly. 'As if I'd made love before,' Teri thought
wonderingly, and knew that loving Sloan had
sharpened instincts she had not even known she
possessed.

'You are so beautiful.' The words seemed to be torn
from his throat.

You are beautiful too, she thought.

He began to kiss her again, her mouth and her eyes,
and then downwards, along her neck to her breasts. As
his lips lingered on each nipple in turn Teri felt dizzy
with desire. No world existed beyond the walls of this
room, the only reality was the sensuous ache that
flooded her limbs.

He lifted her in his arms and carried her to the bed,
and she let him do it. The time for resistance was long
past. There was no longer even the will to resist. She
loved Sloan, and she wanted to experience that love
physically in the way of a mature woman.

What would happen now was inevitable.
Subconsciously perhaps, she had recognised the fact
when she had agreed to inspect Sloan's home with
him. She loved him more than she had thought it was
in her to love any man, and she had hungered to be in
his arms, in his bed.

'I've no shame,' she thought, as she watched him

unbuckle his belt. 'I know there's Miranda, and yet I'm willing to make these moments mine. Perhaps because I know they're the only ones I'll ever have.'

Lying down on the bed beside her, Sloan gathered her to him. He began to kiss her again, to caress her, with a great tenderness this time. A tenderness which was more erotic than anything that had preceded it, for beneath it was the controlled desire and passion of a man.

'I can't wait any more,' he whispered at length, and through a dry throat she said, 'I know.'

Her arms were around his back, she wanted him too. And then as he entered her body pain shot through her, sharp and unexpected, and she jerked on the bed. A cry rose to her lips, but she managed to stifle it.

Sloan stiffened and his body grew still. And then he withdrew from her. Leaving the bed, he went to the window.

Something was wrong, terribly wrong. Teri balled a fist over her mouth to stop herself crying as she watched the tall naked figure, his shoulders rigid.

'Sloan.' It was a whisper.

He did not answer. She whispered again, 'Sloan.' And then, 'What's wrong?'

Without turning he said, 'I hurt you.'

'No—well, just a little. Next time it will be different.'

'Next time!' He wheeled, and his face was so grim that she recoiled.

Miranda. She had forgotten Miranda. Of course—there would be no next time.

'I wouldn't have hurt you if I'd known.' A muscle worked in his jaw. 'Why the hell didn't you tell me you were a virgin?'

She looked at him numbly, unable to answer, wondering why he was so angry.

'Jill isn't your daughter.'

Teri found her voice. 'She's my sister.'

'I see.' Sloan's face went cold. Devoid of any expression. He moved from the window and picked up his trousers. 'I suggest you get dressed, Teri. When you're ready I'll take you back to Vins Doux.'

Emma would have to release her from her promise. There was no way Teri could remain at Vins Doux. Not after what had happened.

On the drive back from Bienvenue she had thought of explaining to Sloan why she had concealed Jill's identity, had in fact tried. But Sloan had been unforthcoming, had made it clear he was not interested, and after a minute Teri decided not to bother. Sloan had had has secrets and seemed not to feel guilty about them. Why should he have a double standard when it came to her own affairs?

She had closed her mouth and lifted her head, before staring out of the window as if she had not a care in the world. Reaching Vins Doux, she had thanked Sloan politely for the interesting day—interesting? it had been devastating!—and then she had pushed past him, past Emma who had come outside on hearing the car, and had made for the haven of her room. There to hurl herself on to the bed, where she had wept until she thought there was not a tear left inside her.

An hour later, looking at herself in the mirror—was this really Teri Malloy, this haggard-faced girl with the haunted eyes and the tear-streaked cheeks?—she had come to a decision. She would leave Vins Doux, promise or no promise. She could not stay here and face seeing Sloan several times every week. Loving him as she did, it would be agony to endure his increased contempt.

Jill was not the child she had brought with her from

Johannesburg. Her face was filled with colour now and the small limbs were growing decidedly chubby. The Cape air and the good food she had been eating agreed with her. It was a shame to take Jill away from Vins Doux. But the move need not be detrimental, Teri reflected. No reason why they should go back to Johannesburg. She would find a job in Cape Town, and with the money she had been able to save while she was at Vins Doux, she would be able to give her sister many of the small luxuries that she had previously had to deny her.

Emma, of course, was an obstacle. It had always seemed to mean very much to the older woman that Teri should stay with her a year. How would she take the sudden decision to leave?

Surprisingly, Emma took it well. She listened quietly as Teri talked.

'I'll miss you,' she said at length.

The grey eyes were understanding. She knows! Teri thought. Holding her breath, she waited for Emma to make some comment on the situation.

Emma only said, 'I'm glad you're not going back to Johannesburg. You'll visit me sometimes, you and Jill?'

'Of course.' But she knew that when she met Emma it would have to be in Cape Town, where there could be no chance meeting with Sloan.

'When were you thinking of leaving?'

Today, if that were possible. But it was not. She must give herself a few days to think, to plan what she would do when she reached the city.

'In a week?'

'Friday? All right, Teri dear. I'll be very sorry to see you go, but I realise I can't force you to stay if that's not what you want.'

Teri thought her head would burst in the days that followed. There was so much to think of, so much to plan. If she had only herself to consider she could face the future with the confidence that somehow things would fall into place. But there was Jill. She had to know that the little girl would have security before she could let herself embark on a new life.

She made phone-calls to libraries and schools and museums. There was no positive offer of a job—she had not expected one so easily—but a few of the responses sounded hopeful, and she made arrangements for interviews.

Teri meant to tell Bruce and Virginia that she was leaving, and found that she could not. The very thought of her imminent departure dried her throat, so that she could not speak.

'I'll just say goodbye when the time comes,' she told Emma.

How would she say goodbye to Sloan? Would she be able to say it at all? Picturing the scene, at night in bed, was no help. Despite all that had happened, the mere thought of saying goodbye to the man she loved made her cry every time.

If only she could avoid running into him before Friday. So far she had been lucky. She had not seen him at Vins Doux. Not that there had been much opportunity. Every spare moment was spent in the library. 'Try to finish researching the section you were busy with,' Emma had said. Even without the request Teri would have done the required work. Emma Roland had shown her only kindness, and she was determined to leave the work in an orderly manner, so that her successor would find it easy to go on with.

'I could continue researching in Cape Town,' she said once. 'I've enjoyed the work so much, I could send you the notes.'

'That's an idea to consider.' Emma paused. 'I wonder if you could do me one last favour?'

'You know I would.'

'I also know you have a lot on your mind right now. Do you think you could look at some books for me, Teri?'

'Of course.'

'You've heard me mention Herman Kruger? No? He was a scholar of some renown once, and he has a fine collection of old books that he wants to dispose of. I've been wanting to lay my hands on them for years.'

'You want me to come with you to see them?'

'I can't get away myself. Not before Friday.'

'I'll go alone, then.'

'Herman's become something of a recluse, he lives in a cottage along the coast. It's not all that easy to find.'

'You could draw me a map,' Teri suggested.

'I'm not sure that I could, and even then you might get lost. Sloan knows the way.'

Teri felt herself grow rigid. 'Sloan will give me directions?'

'He agreed to take you there.'

The colour drained from Teri's cheeks. 'No!' The betraying word was out before she could stop it.

Grey eyes were warm. 'Am I asking too much of you?'

'You know you are,' Teri whispered.

'It's just one day, Teri. You need never see Sloan again after that.' Emma paused a moment. 'The books mean so very much to me.'

The girl drew a shaky breath. 'All right. I'll say goodbye to Sloan at the same time.'

CHAPTER ELEVEN

HE came for her in the morning, and the first moments were awkward. The last time she had seen him had been at Bienvenue, when he'd accused her—he *had* accused her, hadn't he?—of being a virgin, and had told her to dress.

As they drove away from Vins Doux she could not look at him. Just before reaching the highway he stopped the car. Teri was surprised, but even then she didn't turn. Sloan had his own reasons for doing things.

She gasped when fingers touched her hair and two pins were tossed on to the car-seat. She did turn to him then. 'What do you think you're doing!'

'Turning the stern woman into the sweet girl I prefer.'

'You've got a nerve, Sloan!'

'I do? Well, perhaps I have. Worth it in this case, I'd say.' Blue eyes were warm with amusement, and despite herself Teri felt her heart reach out to him.

'This topnotch thing doesn't suit you, Teri.'

She'd known it when she had pinned up the hair and had seen herself stern and aloof in the mirror. Just the right image to wear as an armour, she had thought then.

'I like my hair this way,' she said jerkily.

'Liar,' he responded, but without rancour.

Teri sat very still as more pins were loosened. At length Sloan threaded his hands through her hair, causing it to fall loosely around her shoulders.

'The Teri I know,' he said softly. 'Will you relax now?'

Incredibly, she did. It was a glorious day, with not a trace of the wind that so often lashed the coast. The air smelled of pine-needles and wild flowers, and sky and sea were a vivid blue. Would there ever be a day quite like this one again?

Teri turned to look at Sloan. He looked so handsome that her pulses raced.

He must have felt her looking at him because his head turned and his eyes met hers 'You *are* more relaxed.' He smiled and his hand reached out covered one of hers. 'Let's make this a special day, Teri.'

'All right.' As she smiled back, she knew that she wanted it to be special. Alone with Sloan, away from Miranda and Bruce and Virginia. Away from Vins Doux and Bienvenue. She had made up her mind not to see Sloan again, and yet fate, in the shape of Emma Roland, had intervened. That being the case, she too wanted the day to be special. One last day to add to her precious store of memories.

Did he know that she was leaving? Probably not, for if he did he would surely have mentioned the fact. She would tell him before they returned to Vins Doux, she decided. But not now, not with the day unfolding before them.

Teri had thought that Sloan would be in a hurry to take her to Herman Kruger, so that he could get back to Bienvenue, but such seemed not the case after all. 'Bring a bikini,' he had told her, and she had debated with herself whether to accede to the request. When he drove down to a beach, and the temptation of golden sands and lazy waves lay before her, she was glad she had not been altogether stubborn.

'What happened to the bikini?' Sloan's eyes ran over her as she appeared from the bushes in a one-piece bathing-suit.

She danced him a provocative smile. 'I was taking no chances'

Blue eyes gleamed and mobile lips curved at the corners. 'I suppose you didn't think this slinky piece might be even sexier?' He grinned down at her. 'Come along, Teri, let's try the waves.'

They swam a while, then came out of the ocean and let their wet bodies dry in the sun. Teri lay back on her towel, enjoying the warmth of the sun on her skin. Her eyes were closed so that she did not see Sloan, but she was acutely aware of him.

Presently she opened her eyes and sat up. Sloan looked like some pagan god, she thought, drawing in her breath. Water-darkened hair clung to the bronze-sheened body. His shoulders were broad, his waist and hips narrow, his limbs well-shaped and muscular. Across his cheeks long lashes made a smudged shadow, and his lips were slightly curved, as if he was enjoying some private thought. Teri yearned to touch him, to let her hands explore the hard planes of his body. She put out a hand, let it go within an inch of his chest, then, with a shuddering breath, brought it back to her side.

Without warning his eyes flicked open. For what seemed like eternity blue eyes held green ones. Sloan lifted himself on one elbow, and brushed her throat and one shoulder with his hand. The touch was feather-light. It was also erotic.

He was going to kiss her. It was what she wanted— wanted so very much. I've lost my senses, she thought. This is our last day together and he will end up breaking my heart. But I love this man, and sense doesn't seem to come into it.

He did not kiss her. Instead he said, 'Let's go back to the car and find a place to eat.'

The inn to which he took her was perched high on a

rugged cliff. White-painted tables and chairs stood on weather-worn slate. Clumps of wild flowers grew between the stones, giving the air a lovely spiced scent. Surrounding the cliffs on three sides was the sea, the waves rising only to crash on to the rocks in a ceaseless roar.

Sloan passed the menu over to Teri. 'What will you have?'

'A buttered scone and some tea, please.'

The waitress came, and he gave the order. 'Tea for two, and an ice-cream with plenty of chocolate topping.'

'Sloan!' Teri scolded when the girl had gone. Her forehead was puckered in a frown and her lips were pursed, but her indignation was a sham. It was not possible to be angry with him. Not today.

'You didn't want just the tea.'

'Of course I did. I told you I did.'

'I remember a girl who said the same thing once before, and all the time she was craving ice-cream with all the trimmings. Remember that girl, Teri?'

'Vaguely.' She met his eyes bravely. 'The same girl who said she was experienced in love when in fact she was a virgin.'

'Virginity and a passion for ice-cream.' His eyes shone with laughter. 'Quite a combination!'

'Not very alluring.' There was a catch in her breath.

'Did I say that?'

'No.' Teri did not know what made her add, 'Not like Miranda.'

Something flickered in the blue eyes. 'Not at all like Miranda,' Sloan agreed, and a little of the magic vanished from the day.

The waitress arrived with the tray. For an isolated inn, the ice-cream was unexpectedly good, but Teri could not enjoy it. She made an effort to eat, Sloan would have been both puzzled and disappointed if she had not, but she had no appetite for the confection.

Her throat was thick with the promise of tears. She loved Sloan, she loved him more than she had ever dreamed she could love a man. Yet after today she would not see him again.

Clearly Sloan, who was sipping his tea with evident enjoyment, was not bothered by similar thoughts. It could only be a matter of time till he married Miranda. If he remembered Teri at all, it would be only for her lies and her passion for ice-cream.

The sun was setting when they reached Herman Kruger's cottage. Set well back from the highway, it was on a bumpy unlit road full of torturous bends. Emma had been right, Teri would not have been able to find it alone.

A fierce-looking man with wild white hair and great shaggy eyebrows, Mr Kruger did not seem surprised at the lateness of their arrival. After serving them a thick vegetable soup with cheese and bread, he brought out his books.

They were interesting, Teri saw that at once—first edition volumes which she had not seen before. They would make a wonderful addition to the library at Vins Doux. Herman Kruger was eager to sell, Emma was just as eager to buy, and it was not hard to arrive at a price.

'Do you think you could put us up for the night Mr Kruger?' Sloan asked presently, when the deal had been concluded.

'*Magtig*,' snorted the old man, as Teri jerked round to Sloan with a puzzled look. 'I have just one room, and I don't share it with anybody. Never did, never shall.'

'We wouldn't think of invading your privacy.' Sloan

was sweet reason itself. 'We don't want to put you to any trouble, Mr Kruger, but was that a shack I saw outside?'

'Fishing-shack.' The old man gave a fierce laugh. 'You're welcome to it. Only one bed—should be enough if you two are friends.'

'Mr Kruger, you don't understand,' Teri began, her cheeks warm with embarrassment, only to be interrupted by Sloan, who said crisply, 'Thanks, we'll take it.'

When Sloan had finished packing the books in the car, Herman Kruger gave him a kerosene lamp and some blankets. Heart beating fast, Teri followed him to the shack.

'I don't understand,' she said, as she followed him inside.

Sloan stood the lamp on a small wooden table and turned up the flame. Whistling softly, he looked around him, and Teri looked with him. The shack was small, yet surprisingly clean. There was the faint odour of seaweed, and in one corner was a bundle of nets. There was also a bed. Teri looked at it, and felt hysteria bubble in her throat.

'Sloan! This place!'

'Not bad at all. Herman lets some of his cronies use it when they're fishing this way. These blankets he's given me are clean, we'll just throw them over the bed.'

'We can't sleep here,' she protested over the thundering sound in her ears.

'No place else that I can suggest.' Sloan turned and looked at her consideringly. 'You heard what Herman said, he only has one bedroom. And the bush isn't safe—always a chance of a stray leopard at night.'

'Why don't we drive back?'

'And risk those bends on an unlit road? We could end up in the sea. That would be crazy, Teri.'

Not as crazy as this. I can't share this narrow bed with you, loving you as I do. Knowing that when we awake it will be time to say goodbye.

'There must be somewhere we could stay,' she said at last, slowly. 'The inn where we ate. . . .'

'Miles away. I wouldn't risk it.' He came to her and put his hands on her shoulders. 'Is the idea of sharing a bed with me really so repugnant?'

The idea was sheer bliss, that was the trouble. Beneath his hands her shoulders trembled. 'It's not what I want.'

'You wanted it the other day, at Bienvenue. Or was I mistaken?'

It was not something she could deny. 'No. No, you weren't. But today. . . .' As she put her hands over her eyes she felt her hot cheeks. 'Things have changed. Sloan, don't press me, you don't understand.'

'Perhaps I do.' It was spoken very gently. 'Teri, my dearest, will you feel any better if I promise not to make love to you?'

My dearest. He had used the endearment before, but it meant nothing, it was just his way of addressing a woman. There was only one woman who meant anything to him, and that was Miranda. Any words of real love would be directed at her.

'You don't want to make love?' She stared at him horrified, the words having emerged almost of their own volition.

'I'd love you all night if you'd let me.' His voice had roughened. 'But you'd have to show me you wanted me. I won't force myself on you again, Teri.'

She drew a shaky breath. 'You said something about a promise.'

'You have it.' The roughness had vanished and his tone was smooth. 'Let's get undressed, then.'

'We could sleep in our clothes.'

'And a fine rumpled sight we'd be in the morning! You're not going coy on me, Teri?'

'Of course not.'

She tried to smile as she slipped out of her sundress and saw that his eyes were on her, their expression strange, almost as if he worshipped her body. I'm crazy, she thought. Wearing only bra and briefs, she watched as he took off his own clothes with movements that were suddenly abrupt.

They lay down together on the fisherman's bed. The blankets were rough but clean above and beneath them. The bed was narrow, meant only for one. Teri lay as far to one side as she could, her knees slightly bent, and Sloan lay beside her, shaping his body to fit with hers. One arm went around her. 'To stop us falling out,' he explained.

'I realise that,' said Teri, and felt the long fingers just beneath her breasts, and the warm breath fan the back of her neck.

Presently the sound of slow steady breathing filled the room. Teri lay very still, listening as Sloan slept. She herself would not sleep, she knew, but that was no cause for concern. In the years ahead there would be many lonely nights when she would sleep. For tonight she preferred to lie quietly, with Sloan's arm beneath her breasts and the long length of his body curled around hers.

He would have needed little encouragement to make love to her. As she lay in the dark, aching for him, she wondered if she had been foolish to deny herself the joy that would have accompanied the act. What had stopped her? Not a question of morals. Her love for Sloan transcended principles that had once been iron-clad.

Perhaps there had been the fear that Sloan's lovemaking would spoil any future happiness with another man, that she would never be able to love again. But she would never love again anyway, she knew that with clear certainty. And the moments of fulfilment would have been hers to cherish.

The arm that was curled around her moved slightly, the fingers going to a breast, cupping it, bringing her body closer against his. Teri's breath jerked. 'Sloan,' she said, and then a little louder, 'Sloan!'

There was no response, the breathing was as slow and steady as ever. The movement must have been unconscious.

She lifted her hand to brush his away, then dropped it. She might as well enjoy this closeness to the fullest. This was how they would lie if they were married, night after night of this wonderful intimacy.

But marriage was not for her. There would never be more than this one night. All the others were for Miranda.

She had thought sleep would never come, but presently it did. When she wakened at length, she felt an odd roughness against her cheek and around her almost-bare body, and for a few moments she lay still, wondering if she was dreaming. Suddenly the events of the night came back to her, and her hand moved— only to encounter emptiness.

'Morning, lazybones,' a cheerful voice said.

'Morning, Sloan.'

'Do you always look so rosy-cheeked when you wake up?'

Teri touched her hands to cheeks whose heat was occasioned by something other than sleep. As she did so the blanket slipped away from her. She clutched at it, and an extra warmth flooded her face.

Sloan's laughter echoed through the tiny room. 'Coy again? My darling Teri, I've seen you in less.

Besides, we've just spent a whole night lying together in bed.'

With nothing to show for it. The words came into her mind involuntarily. She thought, Perhaps I'm shameless, but I can't care any longer.

'Do you know,' Sloan went on thoughtfully, 'before I discovered your—innocent status'—wicked grin on the last words—'that coyness would have made me impatient.'

'How do you feel about it now?' She was a little breathless.

'Ah,' he drawled, his grin widening. 'Fancy some coffee before we leave, Teri?'

Why had he avoided the question? 'I'd love some.'

'Good. I'm going over to Herman's, he's offered us his hospitality. Why don't you get dressed and join me there?'

It did not take long to pull on her dress and to run a comb through her tangled hair. Teri shivered as she left the shack and walked the small distance to the cottage. In the room that served as both living-area and kitchen the aroma of strong coffee blended with the smell of freshly baked bread.

'Have a good night?' Herman asked, acknowledging Teri's presence with a lift of shaggy eyebrows.

'Fine, thanks.'

'Thought as much. Indeed. Knew that bed would be big enough for friends.' Looking from Teri to Sloan, the old man gave a grin that revealed that his own memories of the past had not faded.

Teri felt her cheeks go warm again. Involuntarily she glanced at Sloan, and saw his eyes gleam. 'Coffee,' she heard Herman offer, and was glad of the diversion.

Hands curving around the steaming mug, she watched the old man slice a loaf of dark bread. 'Try it,' he invited. 'Always bake my own bread. It's good with *konfyt*.'

When Teri had finished her coffee and the nutty-tasting bread with the sweet watermelon preserve, also home-made, Sloan caught her eye. 'Time to be on our way.'

'Give my best to Emma,' said Herman. 'Nice lady—very nice. And bring your own young lady next time you come this way, Sloan.'

'I certainly will,' said Sloan, but the words gave Teri no joy, for she knew that his future companion would be Miranda. She tried to picture that sophisticated beauty sleeping between the rough blankets of a fisherman's bed and sipping coffee from an earthenware mug, and failed.

Mention of Emma made her feel suddenly remorseful. 'Emma will be worried about us,' she said as they drove away from the cottage.

'I don't think so.' Sloan sounded unperturbed.

'She must be wondering if we've been in an accident.'

'She knows where we are.'

Teri stared at him. 'You phoned her?'

Sloan merely smiled, and Teri knew she had been foolish to imagine that just because Herman Kruger had chosen to live in isolation he had cut off all ties with civilisation. Evidently she had observed neither the telephone nor the moment when Sloan had slipped away to make the call.

'Relax,' he said in a voice that was unexpectedly gentle, and his hand reached across the seat to cover one of hers, briefly. 'Emma knows you're safe with me.'

As I'd always be safe with you. Not the safety of dependence, of wanting a man to smooth my way in the world, to make life easy for me. A different kind of safety altogether. An emotional safety that would come with knowing that I could share my joys and my sorrows with the man I love. Knowing that there is one person in whom I could put all my trust. Knowing that together we could face the world.

Foolish thinking. Dangerous too, for that way there was only heartbreak. With the final goodbye to Sloan just a few hours away, it was madness to indulge in daydreams.

Which brought her to the realisation that she still had not told Sloan of her plans. She should have told him yesterday after all. Now, with the memory of the shared night so poignant in her mind, the thought of the parting made her throat constrict with grief. She did not even know if she could talk. And yet she must do so, she could delay it no longer.

They had driven some way through the awakening peninsula when Teri drew breath and said, 'I have to tell you—I'm leaving Vins Doux.'

No response from the man at her side. Had her voice been so low that he had not heard her? Stealing a glance at the stern profile, she saw that his concentration was on the road ahead.

A little louder this time, she announced, 'I'm leaving Vins Doux.' After a moment she added, 'Tomorrow.'

Still no response. His mouth was tilted in the suggestion of a smile and he had begun to whistle softly.

Clenching her nails hard into her palms, Teri turned to the window. She felt ill. She had not expected that Sloan would agonise over her departure, but his indifference—an indifference that bordered on callousness—was brutal. Tears gathered in her eyes, and she blinked fiercely, determined that she would not cry. But more tears came, till the scenery outside the window was a blur.

Perhaps ten minutes later the car drew to a halt. 'Now we can talk,' she heard a voice say softly.

The time for talking had passed. Keeping her head stiffly averted, Teri resisted the impulse to wipe the tears from her eyes, and hoped that she would not disgrace herself.

'There you have the reason why you won't be leaving Vins Doux,' Sloan told her.

She had no idea what he was talking about, and her swollen throat did not permit questioning.

'Don't you see, Teri?'

Still keeping her face turned away from him, she gave her head a small shake. It was the best she could do.

'I've made you cry.' She had never heard his voice quite so tender. And then he had reached for her, and was dabbing at her eyes with a handkerchief.

'I'm not crying,' she gulped.

'Of course not. Teri my darling, what do you see?'

If only he would not call her darling. To him the endearment meant nothing, and it only made her feel more miserable.

'What do you see?' he persisted.

Nothing. Well, nothing of any consequence. Just a tall white building perched on the cliffs, with a few smaller houses clustered around it.

'A hotel,' he told her.

Later she would wonder why she had not reacted to the word. Perhaps it was a measure of her emotional turmoil that her only response was an almost inaudible 'Well?'

'Well.' Beneath the laughter in his tone there was a suggestion of uncertainty. Sloan, always so self-assured, was uncertain. 'Is that all you have to say?'

'I don't know what else *to* say,' Teri muttered.

'I can't believe that my sleepless night on a narrow bed was in vain.'

'You slept like a log,' she accused.

'I didn't sleep at all.'

'Your breathing. It was so slow. . . .' She lifted her head to look at him, mindless all at once of her tear-filled eyes. 'You were acting?'

'Every minute of the longest night I ever spent. I'm a normal man, my darling. Do you think it was easy to lie beside you without making love to you?'

'Why didn't you?' The words were out before she could stop them. Beneath his gaze she felt her wet cheeks grow warm.

'Because,' he said, very slowly, 'I intend waiting till we're married. If you'll have me, Teri. You and Jill.'

Happiness was a wild thing inside her. 'I don't understand. . . .' It was all she could say.

'Perhaps that's the answer I deserve after all I put you through. I only hope it's not too late. All right, Teri, let's talk.'

'Why didn't we talk yesterday?' she asked wonderingly. We had so much time.'

'Yesterday, my darling, was for wooing.'

'Wooing?' Was it possible to be quite so happy?

'Wooing. Weren't you curious why we took so long to get to Herman? And don't you understand the significance of this hotel?'

Slowly, she *was* beginning to understand. 'We needn't have stayed at Herman's, you knew all the time about the hotel.' And then, 'You planned this!'

'The action of a desperate man. I knew I had to act quickly—get in all my wooing in the space of one day. And one night.'

'A wonderful day. And night.' The small tear-stained face was radiant. 'You said there was nowhere we could stay, and I believed you. I don't remember seeing the hotel yesterday, Sloan.'

'We came along a different road.' Pain filled his

eyes. 'There's so much to explain. *Is* it too late for us, Teri?'

'Go on explaining,' she teased him. It was easy to tease now, with joy exploding like fireworks inside her. She wanted nothing more than to be in his arms, but there were things she had to know.

'I love you,' he said.

'Oh, Sloan, I love you too!'

He was quiet a moment, a dazed look in his eyes, and she knew that he really had been unsure of her. 'I've loved you a long time.'

'But you never trusted me.'

'For a while I didn't.'

'I had the feeling,' Teri said thoughtfully, 'that perhaps you didn't trust women at all, Sloan.'

'So many of the women I'd met were only out to get what they could. Take Virginia—she behaves one way in front of Emma, another way when she's out of her sight. But I think you know that.'

'And you thought I'd conned Emma.'

'You had the face of an angel, beautiful and innocent. I couldn't believe that you'd do anything dishonourable. And yet there were the facts. The expensive clothes. . . .'

'Emma wanted me to have them.'

'I know that now.'

'She told you?'

'Only when I'd made up my own mind about you.'

'Why did she wait so long?'

'She thought that way was best.'

'When *did* you make up your mind?' Teri asked slowly.

'I think I knew all along what you were, my stubborn reasoning notwithstanding. But what finally convinced me was the argument. When you stood up to Emma and told her she had no right to interfere in

Jessie's life. Virginia and Bruce said what they thought Emma wanted to hear. Not you. You were so fearless, my darling, so determined to stick up for what you believed in no matter that you risked Emma's disapproval. That was when I knew the truth.'

'You still thought I was in league with Bruce.'

'The wretched Bruce. He can count himself lucky I didn't do him violence. The thought of you together was enough to drive me crazy!'

'You were right, you know,' Teri said a little sadly. 'Bruce only wanted me because of my share in Vins Doux.'

'He told you that?'

'Indirectly.'

Sloan was watching her intently. 'Do you still feel anything for him?'

'I never did. And I've told you I love *you*.' Odd how easily the words emerged from her lips. She had said them so often, quietly, in the darkness of her room, never dreaming that she would one day say them aloud to the man she adored.

'Just as well. Bruce loves Miranda. He's always loved her.'

'Then why did he . . .?' The words 'go after me' stilled on her tongue. The question was pointless. She knew the answer would be distasteful, it did not need to be put into words.

Sloan spoke at length into the silence. 'I said I'd loved you a long time. But there was Jill. Teri my darling, I never judged you, as you thought I did. But the idea that you had loved, perhaps still loved, another man was one I couldn't bear. And then I came to terms with my feelings. I knew that without you there was no life for me, and I decided that if you'd marry me I'd teach you to love me. Teri darling, I gave you some reasons for bringing you to Bienvenue.'

He paused and gave a wry smile. 'What you don't know is that I was going to ask you to marry me.'

Memory came back, sharp and vivid. Sloan's tight white-faced look when he'd accused her of being a virgin.

'You were so angry.'

'Only because you'd lied to me. And I wondered what else you'd hidden from me.'

'It was a silly lie,' Teri said remorsefully.

'In the circumstances it was justified. Emma says I behaved very badly.'

So they had discussed her. What else had been said? Did it matter? Teri knew suddenly that it did not.

There was one question, however, which did need asking. 'What about Miranda?'

'A good friend, nothing more.'

'That day in the restaurant—I thought you were celebrating your engagement.'

'It's what Bruce thought too. We were concluding a business deal, Teri. I sold Miranda a vineyard she'd been wanting a long time. That's all there was to it.'

Not quite all, Teri thought, remembering the 'hands off Sloan' warning she had once glimpsed in Miranda's eyes. But in the end, perhaps, Miranda would be happier with Bruce than with Sloan. Wisely she did not pursue the subject, and said instead, 'Won't Emma be amazed to hear all that's happened since yesterday.'

Sloan threw back his head and laughed. 'My darling, it's what Emma wanted for us both all along. She knew you were the right girl for me, dear clever lady that she is. She also knew she couldn't make her thoughts too obvious.'

'She kept secrets for both of us.'

'She did. And enjoyed herself immensely.' Sloan's eyes grew thoughtful. 'Fortunately there was a secret she didn't keep.' And as Teri jerked up her head, 'She warned me you were leaving Vins Doux. She'd have told me earlier, but I was away from Bienvenue a few days.'

'Then Emma was in on your plans!'

'Yes, my darling, she was. As was Herman Kruger, who so kindly lent us his fishing-shack when he had a perfectly comfortable spare bedroom.'

'All these scheming acquaintances of mine!' Green eyes danced, but Teri's pulses were racing. 'Perhaps I should go to Cape Town and get away from you all while I can.'

'Don't you dare!' Sloan drew her against his chest, holding her with the kind of tenderness she had yearned for. 'Teri, you have to know, when Emma told me your plans she also let slip one other item of news.

The girl grew still. Intuitively she knew what was coming. 'That I'd refused my share of Vins Doux?'

'Yes.'

'Do you mind?'

'Mind? I'm delighted! I'll still control things at Vins Doux, Emma is seeing to that, but *I* want to be the one to give you and Jill all the good things in life.'

With the impatience of a man who has waited too long for the thing he craves, Sloan's arms tightened, and then he was kissing Teri, deeply, hungrily, as if he would never stop. Winding her arms around his neck and pressing herself closer against his body, Teri kissed him back joyfully, and in her response was much of the passion she had tried so hard to suppress.

At length Sloan lifted his head. 'If you don't want to drive me out of my mind you'll have to marry me very soon,' he said raggedly. 'My God, Teri, you haven't even said you *will* marry me.'

'You know I will, my darling.'

'Have I told you that I love you with every fibre of my being?'

'As I love you. Sloan, let's go and tell Emma and Jill.'

'Not before I kiss you again.'

And very thoroughly he did just that.

ROMANCE

Variety is the spice of romance

Each month, Mills and Boon publish new romances. New stories about people falling in love. A world of variety in romance – from the best writers in the romantic world. Choose from these titles in December.

FORGOTTEN PASSION Penny Jordan
DANGEROUS ENCOUNTER Flora Kidd
EVER AFTER Vanessa James
NEVER TOO LATE Betty Neels
THE LION ROCK Sally Wentworth
STORM IN THE NIGHT Margaret Pargeter
FALKONE'S PROMISE Rebecca Flanders
THE GATES OF RANGITATAU Robyn Donald
SERPENT IN PARADISE Rosemary Carter
REMEMBER ME, MY LOVE Valerie Parv
NO QUIET REFUGE Jessica Steele
FULL CIRCLE Rosemary Hammond

On sale where you buy paperbacks. If you require further information or have any difficulty obtaining them, write to: Mills & Boon Reader Service, PO Box 236, Thornton Road, Croydon, Surrey CR9 3RU, England.

Mills & Boon

the rose of romance

An exciting new look for Mills & Boon.

From January 1984, Mills & Boon paperbacks will appear in these attractive new covers. Look out for them, and be sure of the very best in romance—always.

Mills & Boon
The rose of romance

Rosemary Carter

SERPENT IN PARADISE

After their parents' deaths, Teri had been at her wits'
end as to how best to look after her baby sister Jill
and earn a living at the same time — and it was like
the answer to all her prayers when a chance-met
acquaintance, the elderly Mrs Emma Roland, turned
out to be very wealthy, and offered Teri a job and a
home, on her estate near Cape Town. But Sloan
Garfield took it upon himself to be utterly hostile and
suspicious towards Teri, assuming Jill to be her own
child and accusing Teri of being a gold-digger. But
what business was it of his? And why couldn't Teri
get him out of her mind?

Mills & Boon
Romance for every mood

ISBN 0-263-74446-9

UK £ NET	+000.95

Singapore	$4.25
Malaysia	$4.25
Australia	$2.25*
New Zealand	$2.95

*Recommended

00095

9 780263 744460

All prices are subject to change without prior notice

MILLS & BOON

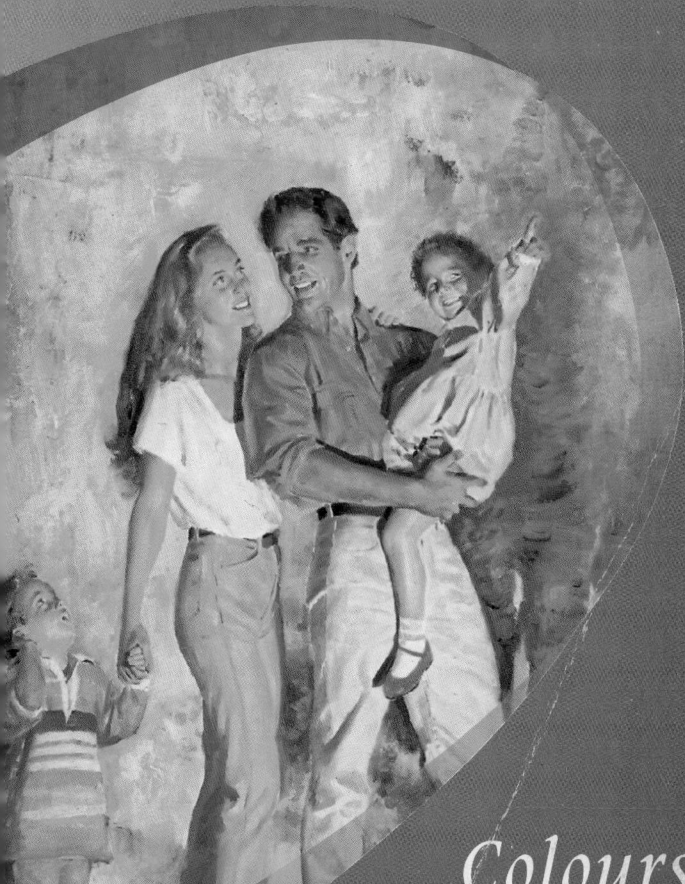

Colours of Love

ROSALIE HENAGHAN